BUTTERFLY

BUTTERFLY

TOMORROW'S CHILDREN

BOOK III OF THE COCOON TRILOGY

DAVID SAPERSTEIN

TALOS PRESS

First Talos Press edition 2014

Talos Press books may be purchased in bulk at special discounts for sales promotion, corporate gifts, fund-raising, or educational purposes. Special editions can also be created to specifications. For details, contact the Special Sales Department, Night Shade Books, 307 West 36th Street, 11th Floor, New York, NY 10018 or info@skyhorsepublishing.com.

Talos Press is an imprint of Skyhorse Publishing, Inc.®, a Delaware corporation.

Visit our website at www.skyhorsepublishing.com.

10 9 8 7 6 5 4 3 2 1

Library of Congress Cataloging-in-Publication Data is available on file.

Print ISBN: 978-1-940456-07-2

Printed in the United States of America

For Ivan, Elizabeth, Ilena, Chaim, Shai, Noa, Eve, Ari, Larry, Sue, Brianna, Rebecca, Ethan, Craig, Gabi, Blake, Chloe, Cori, Barry, Jacob, Zachary, Jonah, Joshua, Eric B., Andrea, Rayna, Benjamin, Eric H., Amy, Dominic, Joseph, Scott, Joanne, Emma, Benjamin, Shana and Joey.

And all my family of butterflies yet to come.

A peaceful, safe and wondrous journey to all.

Other books by David Saperstein

Cocoon—Book I of The Cocoon Trilogy

Metamorphosis: The Cocoon Story Continues—Book II of The Cocoon Trilogy

Fatal Reunion

Red Devil

Green Devil

Dark Again (With George Samerjan)

A Christmas Visitor

A Christmas Passage (With James J. Rush)

A Christmas Gift

Table of Contents

FOREWORD
COCOON

Fifteen years before the start of the Earth's third Christian millennium, after a 5,000-year absence, Antarean space travelers returned to Earth. They were aware that Antares Quad-Three, their once thriving settlement on the continent that some now call Atlantis, had been destroyed by the impact of an asteroid. In fact, just a few islands, the Azores to the east and the Bahamas to the west, were all that remained of the continent above the waters of the Atlantic Ocean. These Antareans found great changes had occurred on the sparkling blue planet. The humanoid inhabitants had emerged from their primitive, tribal, nomadic existence. Socialization, farming, and rapidly developing technology had elevated Earth-humans to a position of planetary dominance.

The once pristine atmosphere of Earth had become hazy and odorous. The protective ozone layer, high above the planet's surface, was being thinned by chemical emissions. This allowed damaging ultra violet radiation from the nearby star to penetrate through the ionosphere and atmosphere to the surface. Much of Earth's life-sustaining water was polluted—some irreparably poisoned. Forests, a major source of the planet's oxygen, were being indiscriminately destroyed at a rate critical to the survival of most life. Gasses emitted by the burning of fossil fuels were raising the planet's temperature to dangerous levels. The polar ice caps were melting. Thousands of species had been obliterated. Thousands more were in danger of extinction. The continued existence of life on Earth was in peril—a fact, the Antareans noted, that was blindly ignored by many of Earth's governments, industries and leaders.

The Antareans were deep-space travelers. Their missions were as traders, teachers and diplomats. In the time before the asteroid's impact that destroyed Antares Quad-Three they had cocooned and secreted a diplomatic army for future use. They believed these soldiers and commanders, numbering nine-hundred forty-one, were secure and safe in a state of suspended animation beneath the sea floor.

But, sadly, the Antareans discovered that pollution and ultraviolet radiation had adversely affected the cocoons, making the life they held partially damaged and dangerously vulnerable. Although the landing party struggled to save their army, unfortunately they did not have the necessary equipment with them to safely process the damaged cocoons.

The Antarean presence was accidentally discovered by a small group of retired humans who mistook the secreted cocoon processing facility for a health spa. The older folks used the facility's equipment and were rejuvenated in remarkable ways. Once discovered, the seniors offered to help the Antareans reseal their damaged cocoons and return them to their underwater chamber, saving the diplomatic army to be revived and awakened in the future.

To show their gratitude, the Antarean leaders invited their aged helpers to join them on their Mothership, and thus become Earth's first deep-space travelers. After much soul-searching the seniors agreed. Clandestinely, the old folks sought out hundreds of their fellow elderly humans who were willing to take part in this unprecedented adventure. With training, the Antareans believed the eager Earth-humans might somehow replace their cocooned army. The volunteers were processed so that their bodies could accept the rigors of extended deep-space travel. They then boarded a Mothership and departed for Antares, a small ice planet orbiting a diminutive star located in the constellation that Earth-humans called Scorpio.

They called themselves The Geriatric Brigade.

METAMORPHOSIS:
The COCOON Story Continues

Five years after the Geriatric Brigade's departure from Earth, a new generation Antarean Mothership, now outfitted with crystalline Parman Guides, an addition that made inter-galactic exploration a possibility, returned. The crew, made up of Antareans and Brigade members, was on a dual mission.

First, to extract the sleeping cocooned Antarean army and bring it home to Antares for controlled processing that would repair and heal the damage done to their cocoons by Earth's pollution and thinning ozone layer.

Second, to deliver a wondrous cargo—twenty-two pregnant Brigade female "seniors," and one young pregnant Penditan bride, to give birth on Earth. The physical processing that had prepared the Geriatric Brigade for deep-space travel had stopped, and then slowly reversed, the physiological mechanics of human aging. The extent of these changes had not been apparent for more than four earth years. So, while fulfilling their duties as diplomats and teachers, the Brigade's reproductive systems re-activated. Some became pregnant, including a few widows and singles who had met and mated with humanoid beings from other planets.

Among deep-space travelers there exists one overriding directive regarding the birth of inter-planetary offspring, especially those of a "mixed mating."

> "All new life to come is a gift. Whenever
> possible, the birth is to be accomplished

upon the home-planet of the mother, or the
egg-bearer, or the divider. The highest
priority of passage is to be given to any
and all travelers who request transport to
home-planet for the purpose of birth. This
right shall be denied to no life form known,
or yet to be contacted, or evolved."

This directive required that these Brigade mothers-to-be return to Earth to give birth. While the cocooned Antarean army was extracted from their secret underwater chamber, the children of the Geriatric Brigade were born.

These unprecedented events were kept secret by directly enlisting the help of the President of the United States, a few of his most trusted advisors, and a devoted team of medical specialists.

After the last baby arrived, a difficult but prudent decision was made to leave most of the newborns secreted and protected on Earth until they reached an age when their ability to survive deep-space travel could be properly evaluated. Three of the children, born of inter-planetary mating, were found to genetically favor their non-Earth parent. It was decided to transport them to that parent's home planet.

Even as infants, it was clear that the children of the Geriatric Brigade were evolved—a new race, possessing new and extraordinary powers. But how these wondrous gifts would effect the children, and their future, was unknown.

BUTTERFLY
Tomorrow's Children

More than fifteen years have now passed since the children of the Geriatric Brigade were born and left behind on Earth. The Third Christian Millennium has begun. The children have been secreted, protected, nourished, educated, and loved at Butterfly House, a private compound on Cayman Brac in the Caribbean—the smallest and most remote of the Cayman Islands.

Aside from their guardians and teachers, and a few trusted people in the United States, no one else on Earth knows of their existence. Most of those who helped in their births believe the children left with their parents on the Antarean Mothership. And of those who know where they live, only a few suspect how very special and talented these children are, or what their potential might be.

But the children know. And the Universe is about to find out!

PROLOGUE

On Earth, our journey into space has been called the final frontier. The adventure began with man observing, and then envying, the bird's ability to fly. From the legend of Icarus; the fertile mind of Leonardo da Vinci; the Wright Brothers first flight at Kitty Hawk; the German V-2 rocket; the Soviet Union's Sputnik circling the Earth; America's Neil Armstrong's walk on the moon; the space shuttle; the international space station; unmanned trips to mars and beyond—humans have been reaching ever upward into space. But the journey has been an agonizingly slow and expensive hit or miss process. The farther we reach the more it requires our will to expend resources and treasure. Many feel we must solve our earthly problems before we aim for the stars, while others think the process of space exploration, and eventual space travel and commerce, will forever unite our planet's human inhabitants. Others believe it is simply our destiny to travel in the universe.

As the Third Christian millennium began, we had taken precious few steps into space since first landing men on the moon. International cooperation was growing, but great leaps forward were held back by our lack of developing new inter-planetary capability, and the frailty of human cargo. Someday, it was hoped, better propulsion systems would be designed to better increase our speed and range. A yet unknown form of suspended animation might enable humans to travel these great distances without aging. All this might take 50, 100, perhaps 200 years. Maybe more. But most believed we would inexorably move out into space. The debate as to whether this was folly, arrogance, extravagance or human destiny rages on.

Optimistic projections put humans on the nearby planets of Mars and Venus by the mid-twenty-first century. Visits to nearby stars, and the solar systems of our own Milky Way Galaxy, might be a reality by the next millennium. But proportionally, these are tiny baby steps into a vast universe whose size and limits are still beyond most understanding.

There is another school of thought that suggests we will go into space as guests of established "alien" space travelers. The hope is that they will share their technology and knowledge altruistically, bringing Earth-humans into space where we would join a vast inter-planetary community of space travelers. Many believe we have already been visited.

But parochial fears and ignorance prefer to portray these alien visits in dark, ominous scenarios. Unearthly space travelers are usually portrayed as aggressive, blood-thirsty aliens, intent on colonization, enslaving us, dining upon our flesh or mindlessly destroying Earth and its population.

Countless books and movies depict violent and pitiless attacks of technically advanced outer-space creatures on an impotent mankind. They show us a universe of gross, fierce, omnipotent non-human creatures filled with blood lust and savage intent.

Those Earth-humans who report they have experienced real-life visitations by beings from outer space consistently maintain they were abducted and then "examined" by grotesque creatures that poked and probed their bodies and minds. The visitors are always labeled as cruel and dangerous. The Geriatric Brigade, and the children of Butterfly House, knew these portrayals were superstitious fantasies conjured out of ignorance, religious fanaticism and fear. Beings from other worlds do not travel through deep-space, across enormous distances, to perform intrusive medical examinations on other species. It was all the nonsense of primitive minds, myths and ignorance.

The Brigade and their offspring understood that the Universe is alive, ordered and functioning—not a place of boogiemen and unfettered evil. There are millions of galaxies, billions of stars, and trillions of planets. Though different in form and substance, life abounds everywhere. Specific existence depends on the physical properties of an environment and the nature of a particular evolutionary process.

The ability to live, function and reproduce is universal. No life is "alien," and of life in the known universe is similar enough to suspect there is a commonality; a genetic link; a universal beginning common to many—perhaps all. Most life is enduring and conscious. To see life across a broad spectrum, as the Antareans and other deep-space travelers do, leads rational thinkers to believe that there exists a grand and intricate plan at work in the Universe. They see a growing, evolving, expanding dynamic process toward an end not yet understood.

To the Brigade, deep-space travel occurred by chance. An accident. The seniors happened to be living in Florida, as retirees, when the Antareans arrived and eventually needed their help. They were in the right place at the right time.

"But was it an accident?" the Brigade's commanders had questioned as they began to assert themselves among many beings and cultures, emerging as leaders.

The Antareans's answer was simple. "Nothing in the Master's Plan is accidental."

Earth-humans were now out in space long before their own evolutionary development and technology might have taken them there. They were traveling, working and breeding among the stars. Their children were very different from other earthly children, evolved far beyond the norm. Their powers were awesome yet their future was uncertain.

If the children of Butterfly House were to leave their home planet, and if they had no contact with Earth again, what might future Earth-human space travelers find in space millennia from now? Would the Brigade still exist? Would their offspring, and generations beyond, have joined the Brigade? Would they be recognizable as Earth-humanoid, or would they have evolved so much that their own species might label them "alien"? And perhaps, as some in the inner circle of the Antarean High Council wondered, might Earth-human space travelers in the distant future find the Universe densely populated with the descendants of Butterfly House?

CHAPTER ONE
IN THE GREAT HALL OF KINNEAR

"**P**lease, you must tell me about the children," Gideon Mersky begged his host, Amos Bright, as they were scanned at the entrance portal to the fabled Antarean Library/Museum. Security had been heightened with the arrival of so many off-planet guests. Clearance for this private, unofficial tour of the facility was cleared at the last minute, after Bright had taken his request to three Secretariats: Arts and Antiquities, Education, and Internal Security. The latter had overriding authority. The other two were involved in the bureaucratic formality that the ex-commander found difficult to abide since his reassignment to Antares.

Amos Bright had been away from his home-planet, Antares, for nearly one Earth millennium. During that time, he had served aboard a variety of Antarean spaceships, rising through the ranks from rookie Astral Navigator/3rd class to Mothership Commander. He was a confident, self-made Antarean, used to making decisions and issuing orders, unfettered. Adjusting to politics and protocol was a classic difficulty faced by deep-space officers returning to home-planet service.

In his new position, as a member of the Antarean Central Council, it appeared that Bright's days of deep-space exploration had ended. He was now officially titled, Lawmaker-Judge and, as such, his life moved at a much slower and more controlled, deliberate pace.

"I'm told that the children are excellent," Bright told Gideon Mersky, as the security scan was completed. The portal seal hummed and began to disengage. "They are prospering far beyond what any of us imagined.

It is rumored that when they put their collective minds together they are capable of wondrous things."

"What does that mean?" Mersky asked, intrigued.

"They seem to be a force unto themselves," Bright mused. "I've heard tell, in council chambers, that some of their parents are disturbed by this phenomenon."

"So when you say 'a force,' how do you mean?" Mersky asked, fighting to mask his overwhelming curiosity from his host.

"Oh...certain capabilities they exhibit individually, and as a group," Bright said vaguely. Mersky was frustrated by the lack of specific information.

"Have they expressed a desire to visit Earth yet?" Mersky asked, looking up at the tall, slender Antarean who towered more than three feet above him. Amos Bright's pale blue robes trimmed with gold thread, signifying his lofty position, were draped loosely across his narrow shoulders and reached down to the floor, accenting his height.

The children in question were the residents of Butterfly House, on the tiny island of Cayman Brac, in the Caribbean Sea, on Earth, 140 light-years from Antares. Gideon Mersky was one of the few Earth-humans who knew about their existence. He was under the impression that they had left Earth with their parents, who were members of the now famed Geriatric Brigade. That information had been withheld on a need-to-know basis. Gideon Mersky had some insight into the children's powers, having been involved with their secret births on Earth, more than fifteen years ago. From the time he saw the children's telepathic powers and their amazing auto-immune systems, he had schemed how he might exploit them for profit.

"No," Bright answered smoothly. He knew where the children were, and he knew Mersky didn't. "To my knowledge they have not asked to visit their home-planet." Bright's answer was glib, giving Mersky the sense that the Antarean was hiding something.

The Antarean processing that had prepared his body for deep-space travel had, as with all the members of the Geriatric Brigade, expanded brain function. But he had not yet mastered telepathic mind reading, so he dared not attempt to probe Bright's thoughts. To do such a thing to an Antarean official would be considered extremely rude, if not criminal.

"I was hoping they might want to go home so that..." His words were interrupted as the Library/Museum's entrance portal cleared with a hiss.

"Ahhh...Here we are," Bright announced, taking advantage of the distraction to end Mersky's probing about the children. "We haven't much time. We can continue this conversation later."

"Of course," Mersky answered as he followed his host through the portal. But he sensed they wouldn't.

The Great Hall of Kinnear was, in a word, dazzling. A ceiling of Chorlian stone, similar in color and texture to a milky, phosphorescent Carrara marble, arched 100 yards above them. Its highly polished, opaque surface absorbed, reflected and magnified the golden light from several Antarean heat-crystal chandeliers that were placed strategically along the rough-hewn, coal-black, Carbonite walls.

The floor, constructed of forged magma, was translucent beneath their sandaled feet. A seemingly endless display of universal wonders, each meticulously presented in its natural setting, spread out before the two visitors. As they moved through the hall, a group of Antarean workers ceased their activities and moved aside, allowing the visitors to pass.

"Dear God," Mersky whispered. "This is overwhelming."

"We've been traveling in space for more than ten of your millennia," Amos Bright replied. "We have made contact with over 900 humanoid life-forms. More than 3,000 additional planets have been scanned, visited and explored. Our discoveries include tens of thousands of species. And now, with our Parman Guides affording us inter-galactic capability, I expect that number will increase geometrically. Our universe is teeming with life, bearing witness to the marvel of our Master's work."

If only they knew on Earth, Mersky thought, as he pondered the impact such knowledge would have on the humans. What would those narrow-minded religious fanatics, whose myopic belief that they alone hold a unique position with God, think about thousands upon thousands of life sustaining planets that were home to untold numbers of civilizations, cultures and religions? How many of those beings, Mersky wondered as he viewed the scope of the hall, were like the Antareans—a civilization steeped in technology that explained many of the mysteries still shrouded in myth and religious dogma on Earth. And yet, he mused, the Antareans seem to possess a deep sense of faith in 'The Master,' who he assumed was their God.

His thoughts were interrupted as a small, bright red, feathered reptile in a nearby display spread its delicately veined white wings and let out a screech that hurt Mersky's ear drums. He jumped back, startled.

"What the hell?" he shouted. Amos Bright, who was walking ahead, looked back to see what had caught his guest's attention. He saw it was the fauna display from Cherriz Adsjar, a planet in the Castor star system.

"Oh yes, Gideon. I know this little fellow personally." Amos smiled. "It is called Pylus." The animal hissed and screeched again. "On Earth it would be described as one of the evolutionary stages between your dinosaurs and birds. This, of course, is a hologram. We do not capture or display live species on Antares. We find the very concept of a zoo intolerable. To remove a species from its habitat and imprison it is an archaic and destructive practice."

As Mersky stepped closer and examined the animal, he could see that it was a three dimensional projection, but as detailed and animated as if it were alive.

"One drop of saliva from a living Pylus and, oh, what's that wonderful Earth expression? Ah, yes,—you're toast!" Amos said with a smile. After two recent trips to Earth, and fifteen years of traveling with members of the Geriatric Brigade, Amos Bright's English was excellent, if a little mid-twentieth in idioms. His teachers were Brigade members whose ages were sixty and beyond, when they had first met. Bright took Mersky by the elbow. "I'm sorry, but we'll have to move along quickly."

Gideon Mersky's eyes could not find a place to rest. Display after display begged for his attention. Much of what he observed in the life forms and species displayed in the Great Hall of Kinnear were, to his human eyes and experience, definitely alien. And yet, though exotic and foreign, in many he found a familiarity that was puzzling. It was as though he had known them from another plane of consciousness, or perhaps in dreams. It might, he mused, be a genetic imprint older than conscious memory. Or perhaps, he thought with a smile, just a side effect of the processing he had undergone for deep-space travel.

"The curators are impatient," Amos Bright said, indicating as he saw, they had interrupted a group of Antareans who, respecting Amos Bright's high rank, impatiently waited to get back to their chores. "They must complete some renovations for the celebration. The Ministries said they are a tad behind schedule. It took all the clout I have to get you in here, but I wanted you to get a sense of the Universe we, and now the Earth-human Geriatric Brigade, know and travel."

"I appreciate that, Amos," Mersky remarked as he stopped and again gazed up at the luminescent ceiling, set seamlessly into the warm, inner-planet stone. "This hall is magnificent. Absolutely awesome."

Bright's thin, silvery lips smiled proudly. Most visitors were initially overwhelmed by the Great Hall of Kinnear. In his own vast travels, he had seen nothing to match its scope and authenticity. He pointed to a new display that was still in the process of being assembled. "This is the area I was keen on your viewing. It's devoted to Earth, and the work of the Brigade." Amos gently took Mersky by the elbow. "You'll get a chance to spend as much time as you wish here later, Gideon. But please do have a look. I'd really like your reaction to it."

Entering Earth's display area, Mersky was impressed with the accuracy of holographic murals picturing the various geographies, topographies, climates, seasons, flora and fauna of his own world. Each contained pertinent sounds, relevant temperatures and specific odors. Realistic presentations of Earth's great cities, and smaller towns and villages, as well as nomadic and solitary lifestyles, were stunningly accurate. A tingle of excitement and anticipation rushed down Mersky's spine as he contemplated bringing some of the perfect presentations of the Antareans' known Universe back to Earth.

The display contained life-like Turlian sculptures of human males, females and children of all races. The Turlians, warm-blooded, carbon-based amphibians, inhabit Cherriz Adsjar, along with Pylus, the creature that had unnerved Mersky, and more than 700 other species.

The main Turlian export is their sculpture art done by incredibly talented artisans whose technique is to create sculptures from the inside out; shaping every organ, skeleton, muscle and circulatory vessel of their subject with uncanny accuracy, adding layer upon layer until the final outer covering, or skin, completes the work. Like many species in the Universe, Turlians chose not to be space travelers. They rely on beings like the Antareans to market their talents and wares.

In another section of the display, all of Earth's languages were integrated into a universal translation programmer—a critical device for space travelers. It contained 1,616 languages, 8,273 dialects, and more than 1,000 electromagnetic synapse conversion programs. Using it, the history and folklore of Earth's civilizations were available to most intra-galactic visitors who might come through the hall. Soon it might be expanded to include information about other galaxies, should their exploration be successful.

The next area contained graphic data on the Earth's natural history. Adjoining it was a hologram explaining Earth-humanoid evolution based on natural selection—a universal process as far as Antarean experience was concerned. The display covered mankind's development from early mammals, through the time of small, hunter-gatherer clans and tribes, up to the current ethnic nation-state structure.

"Is this science of evolution in conflict with the uh, your Master's Grand Plan?" Mersky asked.

"Conflict?" Bright replied, surprised. "What could possibly conflict? The Master forged our universe as it is, as it changes, as it will become. He gave us the task of spreading the word of His grand plan to others. There is no conflict in evolution. All evolves as the Universe unfolds."

"There are many on Earth who believe that God put man on Earth as he is now, that man did not evolve."

"You will excuse me," Amos Bright said politely, "but on Earth you are unaware of the Universe and the myriad life it contains. We once believed as you do. There were priests who used interpretations of the unexplained for power; what you call religion. But as we traveled out into our galaxy, you call it Milky Way, much of the unknown and mysterious was explained, and the priest's dogma was discredited."

Bright's words made Mersky uncomfortable. Beliefs that he held on Earth, anchored in the Born-Again Christian religion, explained cosmic mysteries as God's work, not to be questioned. It defined who would go to heaven and who would not, and why. It gave those who believed a comfortable sense of security in their eternal future and superiority over non-believers. Mersky now looked around him and struggled to grasp the reality of what surrounded him. All that he had been taught to believe was parochial and inconsequential when measured against the display of abundant life and civilizations represented in the Great Hall of Kinnear.

"As you travel with us and the Brigade, you will come to understand that everything evolves. In doing so it has its place in The Master's Grand Plan." Had Bright read his mind, Mersky wondered. "Earth is but a miniscule portion of it," Bright said with a patronizing tone.

Next in the Earth exhibit was a gallery of the famous and infamous Earth-humans and their deeds. The information was remarkably complete and detailed.

"We found you have had your share of tyrants, as most developing civilizations do," Bright told his guest. "Some of yours have been exceptionally brutal."

"Yes," Mersky said softly.

"Our experience is that such beings can delay a civilization's advance for centuries." Bright sensed a feeling of shame in his guest. "Of course you have also had your geniuses to counteract part of that unfortunate waste," he was quick to add.

The Earth display was richer in detail than most of the others in the great hall because the Antareans, who brought the Geriatric Brigade out into deep-space, had once built a huge base on one of Earth's continents—Antares Quad-Three. Millennia after its destruction by the asteroid's impact, humans began to investigate the myths about the existence of the continent they called Atlantis. Although there were many speculations about a lost civilization on Atlantis, no serious scholar ever dreamed it had been a base for off-planet beings. Those few authors and scientists who speculated about this possibility were dismissed as crackpots.

A model of Antares Quad-Three and its diplomatic activities was in the Earth display. Mersky lingered for a moment.

"Atlantis," he muttered.

"Yes. You called it by that name."

"The architecture looks like a mixture of ancient Greek and Egyptian," Mersky remarked as he studied the model of one large city. Many structures featured Ionic and Doric columns with bas-relief facades. Wide stone thoroughfares connected mini-cities scattered along the southern shore of the continent. The largest city on the continent, the one Mersky studied, was situated on a central plateau. A huge pyramid dominated the city's center. Adjacent to the pyramid was a spaceport. Several types of inter-planetary craft were represented, including two Antarean Motherships—the craft that Mersky was familiar with from Amos Bright's last mission to Earth, fifteen years ago. Bright, who was anxious to keep moving, noticed Mersky's interest in the city.

"That city, Ruda, was where travelers from Quad-Three, and deep-space travelers and traders from other quadrants, gathered to exchange goods and information. They negotiated many treaties and alliances there. The Earth's climate and beauty provided an atmosphere where differences were settled peacefully. And there were ancestors of your Greeks on the continent," Bright continued. "They were tribal. Primitive. They kept their distance from us, and," he smiled, "of course we did not disturb their lives either. When we confirmed the asteroid's approach, and point of impact, we moved them to the shores along your Mediterranean Sea. Their memory of our architecture must have remained a strong element in their culture." Mersky gazed at the central city and pyramid.

"Ruda was a beautiful city, Amos."

"Yes, Gideon. It was a difficult loss. But we have learned to acknowledge that there are some universal forces, events and plans that we can neither control nor alter."

"Couldn't you alter the asteroid's course, or blow it up?" Mersky asked, as he studied the model of Ruda, imagining its destruction.

"Blow it up?" Amos Bright was amused. "A popular Earth-human solution to problems." Mersky noted the sarcasm in Bright's voice. "No,

Secretary Mersky, we could not, and would not, blow it up. What if there was life on it? Such cosmic events are part of The Master's Grand Plan too."

The next section of the display contained a graphic, time-lapse laser projection of human reproduction—sexual intercourse, fertilization, gestation and birth.

"There have been several inquiries from under-populated planets regarding the fertility of Earth's inhabitants," Bright explained, as they passed through the display." Noises behind them announced that the workers in the hall were busy again.

"The Brigade is held in very high regard," Bright continued. "Many who were without mates have found companions throughout the galaxy eager to be with them." Mersky recalled his own sexual re-awakenings after being processed for his trip to Antares.

At the time of the last Antarean-Earth mission, Gideon Mersky had been the Secretary of Defense. It was during the presidency of Malcolm Teller. Although at first he had resisted the president's decision to keep the existence of the Antareans, the Brigade, and the children, a closely held, need-to-know secret, Mersky eventually relented to Teller's opinion that it was best to keep it that way for the children's protection. The president was convinced that the world was not ready to accept the concept of a universe containing thousands, perhaps hundreds of thousands of civilizations, many of them far more advanced than those on Earth.

Before Bright and his crew, and those Brigade members who were the children's parents, departed Earth, Bright had promised Mersky he might join the Brigade when he was old enough to be processed. Of course, Mersky was not told that the children, then only newborns, were secretly left behind.

At the age of sixty-eight, Mersky retired from public life. True to his word, Amos Bright made contact with the people guarding and raising the children on Earth. They in turn contacted Mersky through Jack Fischer. Mersky was surprised that Bright had remembered. He was eager to go.

Mersky traveled to Florida with Jack Fischer, the sport-fishing charter captain who had befriended the Antareans years ago. Fischer took Mersky to the island of Eleuthera, in the Bahamas. There, on a moonless, foggy night, they rendezvoused with a shuttle craft that carried Gideon Mersky to the moon's far side, where a Shar-Bakart transport waited. The ship carried a Blanic diplomatic delegation, seven Brigade members who had been serving on Shar-Bakart, and a cargo of chigat bark. The chigat tree evolved uniquely on Shar-Bakart, a nitrogen-water planet in the Pleiades constellation. It had rapid protein repair properties, extremely valuable to the gas dwellers in the Crab Nebula. Now that the Antareans, with their Parman Guides, were beginning to plan inter-galactic trips, other gas-dwellers were sure to be discovered. And so the demand for chigat bark had blossomed. Shar-Bakart transports often made trips to Antares with the valuable cargo.

Although the Brigade members on board were returning to Antares for the gathering, the prospering Shar-Bakart transport owners were happy to make a small detour to Earth for the passenger.

Once on board, Gideon Mersky was successfully processed for deep-space travel, and the transport departed. Although the effects of the processing were at first debilitating, and the journey to Antares arduous, Mersky adjusted and his strength returned. He had not lost interest in sexual activity, even after his wife had lost her battle with breast cancer four years earlier. On rare occasions he had sought female companionship. As the transport sped across the galaxy toward Antares, Mersky felt an adolescent tingling in his groin and a heightened awareness of the female scent. He became interested in one of the Brigade women on the ship. Her name was Annabella Costa, an eighty-three year old widow and former resident of Birmingham, Alabama. The effects of Annabella's deep-space processing were in full bloom. She appeared to be no older than forty and exuded the attractive sexuality of a twenty year old. The prospect of his renewed potency excited Mersky.

"To hell with sexual enhancement pills," he told himself. "I feel like I can get it on au-natural!"

It didn't take much encouragement from Ms. Costa before the two connected. They passed the time enjoying each other with activities both had set aside decades ago, and some that neither had ever explored. Because of the regeneration of their fertility, they took precaution against pregnancy. No Brigade people wanted more babies until they knew the children back on Earth could adapt to deep-space travel.

Annabella, along with all other Brigade members, had been sworn to secrecy about the children being on Earth and their location. Until Mersky officially joined the Brigade, he was considered an outsider, so she did not share the secret with him.

In a separate Geriatric Brigade section of the Earth display, a virtual digital loop of its members, identified by name, rank and status, played continually on a holographic stage. It was devoted to the accomplishments of the Brigade now serving in the far-flung corners of the Milky Way Galaxy.

"I remember you planned to keep our seniors, uh, the Brigade, together to operate the same way as your own cocooned army," Mersky commented. "But in this display, they seem to be separated and spread out."

"Yes." Amos's thin silvery lips turned a pale pink; much like an Earth-human might blush. The tint spread across his pale, Modigliani like, almond-shaped face. His skin glistened. "That was the original concept," he conceded. "But we did not know that much about your kind." Bright bowed deferentially.

"The old folks adapted beautifully to deep-space travel, just as I am sure you will."

"Well, I feel no after-effects, only stronger and uh, younger."

"Precisely. To our surprise, the Brigade people were readily accepted by most beings along our trade routes. Even the Parmans quickly took an immediate liking to them. You see, it's quite rare that humanoids and crystallites relate so well. It became apparent that it would be counter-productive to pursue any plan of keeping them together as a cohesive unit, the way our own cocooned Antarean army had been used."

"Why do you think the Parmans accepted us, uh...them, so readily?" Mersky asked, as he gazed at the hologram.

"Earth-humans were the first non-crystalline contact for the Parmans," Amos explained, "other than Antareans, of course. They observed how your seniors worked so hard to save our cocooned army

DAVID SAPERSTEIN

on our last trip to Earth. Of course, you saw that for yourself. It was that sensitivity, kindness and personal sacrifice that impressed the Parmans."

Amos was referring to the time, fifteen years ago, when the Antareans and certain members of the Geriatric Brigade returned to Earth to remove and rescue the cocooned Antarean army. The mission also brought several pregnant Earth-human women, and one pregnant female Penditan, to give birth on home-planet Earth. The result was the Earth-human children, and one Penditan child, secretly left behind on Earth. Three babies from mixed-mating had been taken to their father's planet where their chances of their survival were deemed better.

"Yes. They were certainly a great help," Mersky agreed.

"As they had been when we first returned for the cocoons, five years earlier," Bright added.

"I heard about that from Jack Fischer. You know, now that I'm sixty-eight, I see how foolish and wasteful it is for society to shun old age. The Brigade members were called 'seniors' and 'retired folks,' and encouraged to disengage from productive society."

"Forced by societal protocol, I'm told," Amos replied. "But they had so much energy, wisdom and knowledge to share. Discarding them was our great gain." Amos smiled inside, to himself.

"So I see," Mersky replied, as he turned back to study the Brigade display again.

"And now that gain, Gideon Mersky, belongs to the Universe. They travel with us. And in their own right, they are leaders!" Mersky's curiosity was tweaked. Had the Geriatric Brigade, his fellow Earth-humans, become that important to the Antareans? "You know my last Earth trip was the first time we successfully used Parmans to guide a Mothership," Amos continued. "That success was a great leap. We then saw that inter-galactic travel was within our grasp. And the bond the Brigade forged with the Parmans made it...well, convenient for them to crew on other intra-galactic missions while our new deep-space craft were being engineered and built." Mersky again sensed something more than just praise in Bright's tone of voice. "No," Bright added, "it was more than convenient. It was the inscrutable work of The Master."

30

Amos Bright's words left no doubt that the Brigade had become extremely valuable to the Antareans. Yet Mersky sensed that the powers and abilities the Brigade had were not completely understood by the Antareans, and so they were attributed to The Master. How far had the Antareans really disengaged from their ancient mystical beliefs?

"They are a valuable addition to the crews that are now are attempting our first inter-galactic travel."

"With the Parmans as guides," Mersky said.

"Yes. They will help deliver the speed required to travel these great distances. The Parmans are a crystalline race who nourish on the ultra-violet end of the spectrum. They extract energy they require from starlight, no matter how distant."

Amos Bright explained to Mersky that this unique ability, coupled with Antarean navigation, engineering and space travel skills had supplied the momentum for the new era of Antarean space travel—inter-galactic exploration. As long as there was an ultra-violet light source, no matter how faint, Parmans could locate its origin and absorb it. The brighter the star, nebula or galaxy, the more energy the Parmans could gather. Thus, as they absorbed cosmic ultra-violet light, they pulled Antarean spacecraft across the Universe.

Albert Einstein's theory of relativity was sometimes explained using the example of a light on a train's locomotive. The train was running at 100 miles per hour. No matter how fast the train goes, Einstein maintained, that light still only traveled at 186,000 miles per second, not 186,000 miles per second, plus the 100 miles per hour the train was making. That theory of light speed was thought to be a universal absolute. Nothing was faster. But his theory was based on light emanating from a source, not a source being absorbed and converted to energy. And because the Parmans were absorbing ultraviolet light that existed in the past, the closer they moved toward the source of that light, the more real-time and intense it became. This phenomenon, named by the Antarean engineers as "Low-end, spectrum/electron, pull-mechanics," enabled Antarean space craft to accelerate toward the selected source until its speed equaled the atomic speed of the ultraviolet electrons the

Parman Guides were absorbing. That speed of absorption eventually approached actual time/space displacement. But once the use of Parman Guides was a reality, it became clear that the existing Antarean spacecraft were not designed to withstand such forces of acceleration. New craft had to be developed.

With Parman Guides on board, all other Antarean deep-space propulsion became obsolete. Intra-galactic time arcs were no longer a constraint. Searches for theoretical time-warp wormholes, and the experimental use of black-hole accelerators, were abandoned. Low-end, spectrum/electron, pull-mechanics enabled the Antareans to possess the ability to jump stars, and it was theorized, other galaxies, all in what might be close to real-time.

Moving at such enormous speed required those travelers, other than crystal-based or hard-carbon based beings, to physically adjust their circulation, pressure/stress capacities and metabolisms accordingly. As the Antareans experimented with Parman Guides within the Milky Way Galaxy, they learned how to control the effects of the new speeds and stresses.

Remarkably, the processing that the Geriatric Brigade had under-gone to make them ideal inter-galactic travelers had also given them the unique ability for intra-galactic travel as well. So they were indeed very important to the Antareans.

"Now there is a new theory our engineers are exploring," Bright told Mersky. "If the Parmans are able to somehow increase their rate of absorption, they might leap across the space-time continuum and thus return to the past."

"Time travel?" Mersky was awed.

"Yes. But it's still just a theory...sort of a secret one at that."

Gideon Mersky had some secrets of his own. After being contacted to fulfill Bright's promise, Mersky had first gone to personal friends—Directors on the Boards of three multi-national corporations. There he revealed what he knew about the Antareans, the Geriatric Brigade, and their children.

"I don't imagine the seniors would want to return home," he had told his corporate partners. "But the children are another matter. The abilities they displayed as infants would be of great use to us. A few drops of their blood could provide the base from which we could build life-extending serums, granting immunity to almost all known disease. And with control over their telepathic and mind-reading capabilities... just imagine?

His proposal garnered the interest and greed of his audience as they pictured reading minds in merger talks, or whispering into the malleable brains of politicians. "And look at all the payoffs and kickbacks we'd save," Mersky added. The potential profits were enormous. In the end, he had made a deal. Now his partners were counting on him to deliver. That meant bringing the children back to Earth. But Mersky knew he would have to be patient for his mission to be successful. At the moment, he had no idea where the children were. Amos Bright, and even Annabella Costa, seemed reluctant to talk about them. Had something gone wrong? Had deep-space travel injured them? Or worse, had they perished? Perhaps later this evening, Mersky thought, I might get a clue from Brigade members who were now gathering for their reunion.

"There's more to see, Secretary Mersky," Bright announced, "and time is fleeting. We'd better shake a leg." Bright moved away from the Earth exhibit. "There's something I want you to see over here." Mersky followed the lanky, graceful Antarean to the next display, a translucent dome that contained a pale blue, gaseous atmosphere. "We'll have to use these," Amos told Mersky, pointing to bulky environmental coveralls and breathing aids hanging outside the display.

"That looks heavy-duty protective," Mersky commented.

"The Subax atmosphere is extremely caustic."

"Subax? Isn't that where Ruth Charnofsky lives?" Mersky asked.

"Yes. In fact, Commander Charnofsky and her mate, Panatoy, arrived on Antares a short while ago. You'll see them later at the reunion." Mersky was pleased. As the Brigade's Chief Commander, Ruth Charnofsky would certainly have information about the children. Mersky was also interested to know how her own offspring, fathered by the Subaxian, Panatoy, was faring. Perhaps the children of mixed-mating might have different potential uses on Earth.

As they donned their coveralls, it dawned on Mersky that there had been no mention of the children in the Brigade exhibit. Not a picture. Not a word. As he pondered why, his fears of failing to deliver the children to his corporate partners on Earth deepened.

CHAPTER TWO
LEFT BEHIND

Butterfly House was a refurbished resort hotel set atop a cliff above a remote cove on Cayman Brac, the smallest and least inhabited of the Cayman Islands. Its neatly shuttered white stucco buildings had faded red, Spanish-style, tile roofs. Four wide verandas, tastefully landscaped, surrounded the main house. The entire compound was concealed from above by tall Date and Coconut Palms, and hidden from the road by thick groves of Mimosa, Banyan trees and Hibiscus hedges.

Few of the ninety, full-time inhabitants of the island, concerned themselves with the Miami banker who had purchased the old hotel for his "clients," about sixteen years ago. They were told it had been bought for a strict Calvinist group who would use it as an exclusive school for the children of wealthy Americans. Caymanians are polite and respectful people. If the occupants of Butterfly House wanted privacy and seclusion, so be it. The natives' silence assured that tourists were kept unaware of its existence.

The facts regarding the residents of Butterfly House were quite different from their cover story. For more than fifteen years, it had been the home, school and secret haven for a group of very special children, their guardians and teachers.

The oldest of the children, Melody Messina, had been born in deep-space, aboard an Antarean Mothership as it sped toward Earth. Seven minutes after her birth, the Erhardt twins, Joshua and Eric, arrived in the Universe. The rest of the twenty-two children, now in residence, had been born in top-secret Building Eleven at NASA's Johnson Space Center, in Houston, Texas. Although they were now chronologically nearly sixteen Earth-years old, physically the children appeared to be more like twenty. They were taller than average—six feet or more. Their bodies were fully developed, and there was no Earthly measurement capable of accurately judging their intellectual capacity.

When these twenty-two children had been secreted in Butterfly House as infants, three of their peers had been taken into space, because they genetically favored their off-planet fathers.

All of the Butterfly House children were the progeny of parents who had once lived in South Florida as "senior citizens," and had chosen to leave the planet with Antareans. What they chose was a long and useful life traveling, teaching and serving as diplomats. Known as the Geriatric Brigade, they had traveled to stars, planets, moons and asteroids in all Quadrants, or Quads, of the galaxy. Now, they were about to begin crewing new Antarean spacecraft designed to explore other galaxies.

The children were protected, nurtured, educated and raised by the few who knew their origins. But now, as they reached maturity, even their guardians did not fully understand all of the powers they possessed.

Individually, and collectively, the children understood their special talents and gifts. They could read the thoughts of others, and thus potentially influence actions and behavior. They communicated verbally and telepathically with one another, and with some species on Earth—mostly marine mammals and simians. They were also able to gather, process and assimilate huge amounts of data instantly. All were aware that these powers came from an inborn genetic ability buried deep within their central nervous systems and brains. As they aged, they discovered that aside from their parents in the Brigade, this ability was highly developed and functioning in many extra-terrestrial species. During the past several years, children of Butterfly House had developed and honed these powers, reaching out across the galaxy telepathically, in a language whose base was a mixture of pure thought and emotion. If the powers lay dormant in a species, they were capable of being activated by the children. All but three of the children had Earth-humanoid parents now off-planet serving in the Brigade. Those three were children born to Peter Martindale, a retired steel worker/union official, and his wife, Tern, a Penditan huntress whose home was a lush, tropical, oxygen-water planet called Turmoline—the fifth planet orbiting the star Spica in the constellation Virgo, located in Quad-one of Earth's galaxy.

Three years ago, the children of the Geriatric Brigade began to express a desire to leave Cayman Brac and visit other parts of Earth. Although everything they needed for their education was available at Butterfly House, and they understood the need for absolute secrecy regarding their existence, they yearned for interaction with people beyond their secret enclave.

"We are human beings. This is our planet. And yet we have never met anyone in person besides our guardians and teachers. We have read about places and peoples. Now we want to see them. We want to know them." The children were adamant. When their guardians resisted, the children responded by cutting off telepathic access to their thoughts. Even Bernie and Rose Lewis, the two Brigade members who had remained behind with the children, were unable to enter their sealed minds. Bernie Lewis, a Brigade Commander with highly developed telepathic powers, marveled at the abilities the children possessed, which were beyond his own. He relented.

Under the guise of furthering the children's education, birth certificates, high school transcripts, SAT scores and extra curricular records were created. Applications were made to colleges and universities in several countries. All the children were accepted. So, as the Third Christian millennium was underway, the children spread out across the world to explore and learn. Alone, or in twos and threes, they traveled their home planet. Among the common people of the world they discovered a deep yearning for peace, harmony and freedom. They saw the evil of corruption, fascism, dictatorship, greed and fanatical religious fervor that caused human misery. Most people wanted a better world for their children. With their abilities, the children of Butterfly House might have played a part in aiding a behavioral turn-around of humankind. But they did not interfere; at least not at this point in time.

When they returned to Butterfly House, the children no longer allowed their self-knowledge, thought processes, or intellectual capacity to be measured. Most of their days were spent sequestered as a group. At night, secluded and apart from their guardians and teachers, their activities were a mystery. No one, including Rose and Bernie Lewis, knew why they were behaving this way. Rose feared that the children, offspring of genetically changed parents, might be somehow damaged or ill. Bernie Lewis felt otherwise. His concern was with what the children might be secretly planning.

CHAPTER THREE
THE SLOOR OF KLANE

The daylight on Klane was a deep red hue—the result of the rising of its sun, a Red-Giant that was the huge planet's primary energy source. Daytime lasted the duration of five and one half Earth days and nights. To be exact, 132 hours, 27 minutes, 44 seconds. Klane's orbit was circular.

Every planet that the Antareans had discovered and explored had its own unique size, gravitational pull, density, magnetic field, atmosphere, energy source, core, orbit, rotation and tilt. The Antareans calculated and recorded light and dark periods—the day/night cycles of a planet. They then converted them into Antarean-time. But in the early days of Brigade travel, Earth-time was also calculated as a comfort tool for the Earth-humans. That practice had been abandoned after a few years, as the Brigade became seasoned space travelers.

As Klane's sun, bearing the Antarean label, Big Red-1104-Quad 7, disappeared below the planet's featureless horizon, an inky black veil, set with a glittering array of celestial bodies and cosmic dust, illuminated the sky. The topography of the planet where the Antareans and Brigade were working was flat, consisting of porous rock dappled with a seemingly endless variety of lichens. A vast milky-gray ocean surrounded them. The liquid was an oily substance that, depending on subterranean volcanic activity, varied from sixty to seventy-three percent ammonium hydroxide and potassium fluoride, suspended in equal parts of water and hydrogen peroxide. To the visitors, it was a very salty, poisonous substance. The ocean, which covered more than half the planet's surface, was nutrient-rich with thousands of yet unclassified photo-plankton and zooplankton species ranging in size from microscopic to over a foot in length. Several sections of this hemisphere had been charted by the orbiting Mothership. In some places it recorded ocean depths of more than two miles. There were other aquatic pelagic species, but very few as yet classified land animals, all of which were reptilian. So far, no mammalian life, humanoid or other, had been discovered.

The atmosphere of the planet was extremely caustic for the visitors. Protective clothing and breathing devices were required when working outside the Mothership, which was parked on the porous, rocky shoreline.

The dominant inhabitants of Klane were a batrachian species called Sloor. At the moment, they were hibernating in the deepest, darkest chasms of the ocean. They were intelligent and potentially communicative amphibians. Little was known about their life cycle and societal organization.

Once every cycle, on its journey around its Red-Giant star, Klane came in close proximity, 67,836 nautical miles, to its largest moon. Brigade Commander Alma Finley, had named it Jade, as it had a deep green coloration—a sure sign of rich copper deposits. As these two celestial bodies approached one another, the gravitational pull was enough to cause Klane's axis to tip. That phenomenon lowered the atmospheric temperature and created conditions that triggered the Sloor to end their hibernation under the ocean and emerge onto the land. As that time now approached, the Antareans and Brigade members made plans to attempt direct contact with the Sloor.

The discovery of the Sloor had occurred eight Antarean years ago when a Mothership, commanded by Amos Bright, was on an exploration mission to this far quadrant of the galaxy, and identified Klane as a life-bearing planet. A landing party made a brief sighting of a few Sloor who were the last to begin hibernation. It was from a distance and the visitors had been unobserved.

A second trip to Klane, led by then newly promoted Antarean female Commander Beam, was four Earth-years ago. It happened to coincide with the Sloor emergence. Still at a distance, certain changes in the new generation of Sloor were noted. The young had the ability to walk upright on their hind legs. Their parents, like most amphibians, still walked on four legs. Both the youth and adults were capable of flight. The lungs and circulatory systems of the new offspring were measured to be proportionally larger than their parents. They seemed to function more like warm-blooded creatures. These measurable and visible evolutionary changes, some that normally might take hundreds of generations on most planets, seemed to be occurring on Klane with amazing rapidity.

On this current trip, the third to Klane, the investigative, scientific and diplomatic teams included six Antareans, again commanded by Beam, and thirty-eight Geriatric Brigade members, led by commanders Joe and Alma Finley.

In their former life on Earth, the Finleys had resided in Boston, Massachusetts, and retired to Coral Gables, Florida, where they were among the first to make contact with Antareans. Also in the group were Paul and Marie Amato, formerly of St. Louis, Missouri, and Boca Raton, Florida. Their daughter, Beam Amato, now a resident of Butterfly House, was named in honor of their current Antarean commander, Beam.

Antarean communication within the galaxy moved at light speed through a series of transmitters and boosters erected on several planets, moons and asteroids in every Quad. They were designed to route communications back to Antares, or to Motherships, via the most direct line-of-sight path possible. But a time lag was inevitable. Instant communication was impossible. Now, with missions hoping to expand to other galaxies, the distances that inter-galactic messages would have had to travel were far beyond any communication technology the Antareans possessed.

Initially, communication between Butterfly House and the Brigade had been done via the existing Antarean transmitter links. But as the children settled into their life on Cayman Brac, and the Brigade moved out into the galaxy with the Antareans, a new form of communication had slowly emerged among the Brigade Commanders. It began with Chief Commander Ruth Charnofsky, and the Finleys. It mystified the Antareans. These three Earth-humanoid commanders, and eventually the other Brigade commanders, were able to communicate with one another using a new form of telepathy—a feat that the Antareans were unable to copy. The Brigade commanders were not sure how it actually worked, other than it required an "act of faith," as Ruth Charnofsky explained.

"We have learned to listen to an inner voice," Ruth told Amos Bright, as they returned from the Chimer planetary system in Quad-nine, after a nearly disastrous encounter with a comet that had inexplicably moved out of its projected orbit. There were other Motherships in the Quadrant with Brigade commanders on board. While the Antarean communications officer sent a warning message over normal channels, Ruth Charnofsky was able to contact the Finleys instantaneously. It was a startling discovery. "We can detect a message sent by one of our commanders as thoughts suspended in time and place. The communication is immediate in terms of the sense, but not the details, of the message. Its presence is "felt" by the other commanders. Acknowledgement of its existence, and therefore its reception, takes what we call, an act of faith. Once the message is sensed, and accepted, we are able to understand it in its entirety. And, it seems to work from any distance." What Ruth Charnofsky did not reveal to the Antareans was that the children of Butterfly House also possessed this ability.

Other than their unswerving belief in a grand cosmic plan at work in the Universe, a plan devised by an entity they called The Master, the Antareans were a technologically based society. They believed The Master had designed all universal matter, movement, change, action and reaction. They had developed incredible science with, what they imagined, were irrefutable laws. For them to accept any new or contrary physical laws, they had to be scientifically proven. The energy source that powered the Brigade commanders' instant long-distance communication abilities evaded scientific identification. Yet, the fact could not be challenged— intra-galactic telepathy between Brigade commanders worked.

Spurred on to identify and isolate the energy source of this new capability, some Antarean scientists suspected that a quantum leap in space travel had occurred, something beyond their new generation of Parman guided inter-galactic Motherships. They secretly reported to their High Council that they were encouraged enough to pursue the highly theoretical concept of thought-travel—sending and receiving messages and visuals from the very limits of the universe, if in fact, such limits existed.

But now, with Parman-guided Antarean voyages out of the galaxy imminent, communication with the Antarean home base would be critical once the inter-galactic journey was accomplished. The newly discovered Brigade commanders' telepathic powers were taken as a sign from The Master that inter-galactic travel was meant to be, and the Antareans were to be the first of their galaxy to do it. The High Council ordered that all Antarean inter-galactic Motherships were to have at least one Brigade commander on board. Since there were only nine such commanders in space, the tenth being Bernie Lewis on Cayman Brac, their availability had become the highest priority.

It was the end of the fifth day-cycle on Klane. The Amatos had chosen to be trained as biologists. The Sloor fell within their area of expertise, so they were the lead Brigade scientists on this project.

In her laboratory aboard the Mothership, Marie Amato worked on the chemical content of the latest sample of fluid extracted from the depths of the nearby ocean. Commander Alma Finley entered the laboratory, bursting with excitement.

"Great news!" she announced.

"What?" asked a startled Marie Amato, looking up from her Molex-scope, an Antarean version of the electron microscope.

"Ruth has arrived on Antares for the gathering. She left me a wonderful thought." The way they described their new communication power was likened to picking up a gift. "There's to be a mission to Earth!"

"Home?" Marie gasped.

"She's going to request that the children be tested," Alma continued. "To see if they are ready to join us!" Marie Amato's eyes filled with tears. It had been nearly sixteen years since she had seen her baby, her little Beam.

"Ruth's on Antares?" she asked, finally focusing on what Alma had said.

"For the gathering, Dear."

"Of course. I forgot. When are they going? Who is going?"

"Soon," Alma answered as she moved to Marie's side. "The Greens and Perlmans will want to go for sure, plus an Antarean science team. They're taking one of the new generation Motherships." Marie stood up.

"Those ships are equipped with Earth atmospheres!" she said excitedly.

"Exactly."

"That means they plan to take the children off-planet!" She embraced Alma. "Oh, dear God! My baby is coming to me!"

At that moment, Paul Amato entered the lab carrying a sample of fresh lichen spores.

"Who's coming where?" he asked. Marie ran to her husband.

"Beam! Our darling Beam is coming to us!"

"Hold on a minute," Alma said softly. "I didn't say they were coming just yet. They have to be tested and..."

"But a new Mothership?" Marie interrupted. "You said they were sending a new Mothership and four Brigade commanders—Ben and Mary Green, and Abe and Bess Perlman. That's got to mean they plan to evacuate everyone." Marie paused in her excitement as a thought crossed her mind. "Of course, first they'll have to test the children. Oh dear...What if they can't travel?" Paul put his arm around Marie's shoulder. She was always highly emotional—a good trait when encountering new species, but a difficult one when disappointment loomed.

"Just put that thought out of your mind, Sweetheart. I'm sure they're going to pass the tests with flying colors," he assured his wife.

"No doubt," Alma Finley added, trying to cheer the doubtful Marie Amato.

"You really think so?" Marie asked hopefully.

"I surely do. They're extraordinary kids. Bernie says that in many ways they possess abilities beyond the Antarean Council's expectations."

"Then the Ants will want to use them," Marie said with contempt. "Ants" was a euphemism the Brigade had given to the Antareans. Of course, it was never used in their presence.

"From what I've gathered from Bernie," Alma said smiling, "no one will ever 'use them,' unless they want to be used."

Marie and Paul nodded. "Bernie says they're quite a force, with a strong collective mind of their own." Her words gave the Amatos pause. They realized they didn't really know very much about their daughter, or the other children. After a long awkward moment, Alma Finley changed the subject. "So? How goes the work?"

Paul removed his arm from around his wife's shoulder and placed the latest sample on the work bench.

"The temperature is rising. The lichen spores are metamorphosing again," he said.

"And the ammonia content of the sea has dropped another six percent," Marie added. "It has been dropping consistently during the last four daylight periods. At this rate, the emergence may be sooner than we anticipated." That was exciting news. If true, Alma Finley had to accelerate the expedition's greeting preparations.

"How much sooner?" she asked.

"Depending on the lichen activity, I'd say half the time we estimated," Paul answered.

"Maybe less," Marie said softly.

"But that could be only a month."

"Or less," Paul muttered, as he examined his new samples under the Molex-scope. "It appears the lichens have accelerated again."

Alma Finley was concerned. A member of the Antarean High Council was supposed to be present at this emergence. She would have to inform Antarean Commander Beam immediately. But what if the expedition was ready to leave for Earth? Or maybe the gathering had concluded? Would there be a Mothership free to travel to Klane with the chosen Council member? With inter-galactic travel imminent, the new fleet had been committed to those missions. Two new Motherships, with Brigade commanders Frank Hankinson and Betty Franklin aboard, were going on separate missions—the first attempts across the great void to galaxies as yet unnamed. Alma Finley's thoughts reached out to her commander husband, Joe, who was outside, fifty-six kilometers to the east of the Mothership's laboratory.

"We're spread pretty thin," she communicated, after informing him of the Earth-mission and lichen changes.

"Something big is up, Alma," he told her. "I've sensed it all through this last daylight period."

"You mean with the Sloor?"

"Yes. And on Antares and Earth. And there's more." His voice sounded concerned.

"The children?" she asked.

"No. At least I don't think so."

"Then what?"

"It's just...well, I've had no actual messages from Frank or Betty, but I know they will complete the test flights on the new Motherships shortly and request clearance to make their inter-galactic jumps. I sense a surge of something. An activity I can't define."

"What does it feel like?" his wife asked. Joe had the gift of great sensitivity even before the Antarean processing for their departure from Earth.

"Radical changes. Evolutionary accelerations. Like we observed here four years ago. But more. And not just here..." Joe Finley was a solid, level-headed man. He did not frighten easily, nor panic. But there was an uneasiness in his voice that Alma did not like.

"Are you okay, Joe?"

"Me? Oh yeah. No sweat. After I take one more measurement, I'm coming in."

Later, in the daylight time-period, an excited Joe Finley entered his shuttlecraft, anxious to meet with the others at home base to discuss the sensation that troubled him. As he lifted off the beach, banked, and headed toward the Mothership, he did not notice the slight agitation on the gray oily surface of the sea nearby. As he sped away, it grew in intensity.

CHAPTER FOUR
BEFORE THE HIGH COUNCIL CALLS

More than 400 of the original 941 Geriatric Brigade members were on Antares, for the gathering. The rest were working on various planets across the galaxy. The reunion brought old friends together after missions that had separated some of them by hundreds of light years. Most had not seen one another for more than an Earth-decade. They embraced joyously and excitedly exchanged information about the wonders they had seen. Those who had traveled the farthest from Antares marveled at how vast the Milky Way Galaxy was, and at the fact that it was only a tiny part of the Universe.

All were healthy and vigorous, showing no signs of aging. In fact, they appeared years younger than they had when they first left Earth. Word of the Brigade's endurance, wisdom, kindness and fertility had spread across the galaxy. Several widows and widowers had mated with, or married, humanoids from planets in distant systems.

The main topic of conversation was about the children, a subject the Brigade spoke about only among themselves, and always in hushed tones. There was an electrifying rumor of an impending trip to Earth to test the children. Everyone hoped for a positive outcome that would allow the children to leave Earth safely. The Brigade members whose children were at Butterfly House could hardly contain themselves, knowing they might soon have their children with them. Many who wanted to start families of their own were also anxious to know the children's test results. If all was well, and the children were able to space-travel now, the voluntary hiatus on conception among Brigade members, or with beings from other planets, would be lifted.

Few had experienced difficulty in adapting to intra-galactic travel and exploration. All were aware that the Antareans valued the Brigade's presence on their Motherships, especially when exploration of new star systems and planets was involved. In fact, among all space-traveling beings, it was often discussed that the Antarean facility for intra-galactic exploration and trade had increased greatly because of the Geriatric Brigade. It was also rumored, now that inter-galactic exploration might soon begin, that the Parman Guides would not cooperate unless Brigade members were on board—a development said to be quite troubling to the more conservative Antarean High Council members.

Excitement reached a peak with the arrival of the Brigade's chief commander, Ruth Charnofsky, and her Subaxian mate, Panatoy. The celebrated couple had been working with forty Brigade members in the Harati System, with a carbon based simian life form called Chula. While traveling from the Harati System to Antares, they had stopped at their home on Rigal Quad-four, in Andromeda, to visit their daughter, Autumn. She had been born on Earth, but was transported to Rigal because she was genetically 89% Subaxian and therefore required the atmosphere and ultraviolet light on that planet to thrive. Ruth's and Panatoy's arrival on Antares signaled that the gathering was about to officially begin.

While Brigade members renewed old acquaintances, the first order of business for the commanders was to report to the Antarean High Council. Ruth Charnofsky, Ben and Mary Green, and Arthur and Bess Perlman were the only Brigade commanders present for the gathering. Joe and Alma Finley were on Klane, awaiting the emergence of the Sloor. Commander Betty Franklin was on the shakedown cruise of a new generation Mothership, and if all went well, would be on her way to explore another galaxy. The same was true of Commander Frank Hankinson. His Mothership, should it prove worthy, would travel across the vast, deep void to a second chosen galaxy. Bernie Lewis, the tenth commander, was ensconced at Butterfly House with the children. While the five Brigade commanders were in an anteroom waiting to be called into the High Council meeting, Ruth Charnofsky informed the others that she had sent a message to Cayman Brac regarding the proposed trip to Earth.

After their hurried tour of the Great Hall of Kinnear, Amos Bright escorted Gideon Mersky back to his guest quarters, promising to pick him up later and personally escort him to the dinner and festivities. Bright then hurriedly changed into official robes to attend the High Council meeting. He was late because, in deference to the Brigade gathering, the council had adjusted their planetary time to Earth days and nights which were much shorter than Antares time periods which were based on their underground life near their ice planet's core. Above ground, Antarean days were nearly three times longer than Earth's. But now, everything operated temporarily at twelve hours of darkness and twelve hours of artificial Earth daylight. This bright illumination and time change was disconcerting for most Antareans, especially those like Amos Bright who had not been in space with Earth-humans for a while.

Amos Bright rushed to the council anteroom to meet with the five Brigade commanders before the council convened. He had briefly greeted the Greens and Perlmans when they had arrived the day before yesterday, but he had not yet seen Ruth Charnofsky.

"You look radiant," he told the feisty, red-haired commander as he entered the anteroom. Her smooth, high cheek bones and doe-like eyes now seemed unearthly to him. Her trim, athletic body belied her age— eighty-six Earth years. Ruth's pigmentation showed traces of pale blue, indicating that she was somehow adapting to the ultraviolet energy sources from Rigal, and becoming more Subaxian. It made Amos Bright uneasy to see this Earth-human adaptability.

Ruth Charnofsky greeted the tall Antarean with a genuine hug. Her strong arms fit easily around Bright's narrow torso. He accepted her embrace gracefully, although this kind of display always made him nervous. It was very un-Antarean. They were a race known for deferential manners and minimum physical contact.

"And you, Amos Bright, are still a charming liar," Ruth told him. She smiled broadly and released his stiffened body from her clutches. "It's so good to see you! Imagine...a High Council member!"

"Yes. But one who aches to travel." He paused for a moment as a touch of melancholy moved across his smooth, hairless iridescent face and brow. Then he grinned. "Ahhhh...But it is so good to see you all together. How long has it been?"

"Almost seven years since Mary and I last saw you," Ben Green said.

"Nine for us," Art Perlman chimed in.

"More than five for Panatoy and me," Ruth added. Many in the Brigade had not yet completely accepted the projected longevity the Antarean deep-space processing had given them. Five or nine years still felt like a long time. But to Antareans, whose life span was indefinite, these time-measurements were insignificant. Bright shrugged and smiled.

"How is that little girl of yours, Ruth? How is dear Autumn?"

"Totally her father's daughter, thank you. From the moment she was born. And not so little, as you may recall." They all remembered how Autumn had grown quite large in Ruth's womb, especially as she approached term. The baby's long Subaxian arms and legs had extended to the point where they were a threat to Ruth's spine. Delicate in-utero surgery had been performed to ease the pressure. Shortly afterwards, Autumn arrived via cesarean section. She was the last of the Brigade children to be born on Earth. Autumn, and two other male children of mixed mating were genetically more like their non-Earth-humanoid fathers and so were taken to that parent's home planet.

One mother was Ellie-Mae Boyd, a Black retired nurse from Charlotte, North Carolina, who had been working at the nursing home where Betty Franklin, Bess Perlman's sister, had been vegetating before being whisked away and processed for space travel. Ellie-Mae's baby's father, Dr. Manterid, was a Hillet from the planet Betch. He was a master chemist with a galactic reputation. Physically, their son looked Earth-humanoid. He bore none of his father's striated markings or thick layered skin. But at birth, doctors discovered that this newborn required the nearly one hundred percent nitrogen atmosphere of Dr. Manterid's home planet.

The other baby was the son of Brigade member Karen Moreno, and a farmer named Tommachkikla, who hailed from the planet

Destero—a huge, hot, oxygen rich planet in Orion. Tom, as he was called, was pure humanoid. Destero's sun, the middle star in Orion's belt, is similar to the Earth's sun in size and age. The planet's age and distance from its sun is also similar to Earth. But because of its size, Destero's gravity is nearly ten times stronger. Humanoid inhabitants there have evolved into a race of short, squat, powerful beings with small lung capacity. The Desterian's main occupations in the planet's harsh environment are farming and mining. The child needed an oxygen rich environment. He had difficulty breathing Earth's mixed oxygen-nitrogen atmosphere so he was brought to Destero.

Although there was fear that these three babies might not survive the trip from Earth to Antares, and then on to Subax, Betch and Destero, the risk was far outweighed by the certainty that they could not survive on Earth without constructing elaborate isolation chambers to provide controlled atmospherics, pressures and temperatures. Building habitats that complex would have surely increased the risk of someone discovering the secret of Butterfly House.

The Antareans insisted they would not chance deep-space travel for these babies without some form of processing. They had applied one fifth of Panatoy's processing regimen to his daughter, and the same for Dr. Manterid's son. The Desteran child was given more because of his bulk, dense muscle and bone structure. Autumn, Ruth and Panatoy's daughter took the processing well, as did the Desteran. But it affected Dr. Manterid's son adversely, and he nearly died. Fortunately, they were able to make adjustments before the processing did permanent damage to the infant. In the end, the three children survived the trip beautifully—a positive foreshadowing for the children left behind on Cayman Brac. Since that time, the three had not left their fathers' home planets. However, these children were in telepathic contact with the children of Butterfly House.

"Autumn nearly killed me in my womb and now she drives me crazy outside of it," Ruth Charnofsky told Amos Bright.

"The young are mostly the same everywhere," Amos commented.

"But not on Antares," Ben Green piped in. "Your kids are extremely well behaved." Ben, a tall heavyset man, now in his late seventies, looked no older than forty. The manifestations of age and aging among Brigade members could no longer be described in Earth years. They were vigorous and seemingly ageless. Ben was muscular; with a deep tan he'd gotten on Turmoline during a recent Penditan trade mission. His once gray hair had reverted to its original sandy blonde. He styled it in a buzz cut. His pale blue eyes were keenly alert—a commander through and through.

"That is because we choose to raise them institutionally," Amos Bright answered. "No parents to distract them or blame for their short-comings." Antareans had long ago become asexual. Eventually they lost their reproductive drive and, finally, most of the function of their reproductive organs. But they kept the male-female distinction for tradition's sake. They had no sense of family, in the Earth-human way. They now reproduced via cloning techniques developed millennia ago. Only when an Antarean was accidentally killed, or chose to die, was another cloned in his, or her, image. They were brought to term in vitro. The young were exact genetic replicas of the parent, with improvements added as their genetic sciences progressed. They retained a base amount of their parent's imprinted memory, but most of their brain capacity was a clean slate upon which the Antarean State inscribed their life-plan. Antareans raised and nourished the young, then trained them for their careers. Many were devoted space travelers, explorers and traders. Basic to the plan was the inculcation that Antareans were a chosen race; their mission—to serve The Master and his Grand Plan.

"But being a part of a child's discovering life's possibilities," Mary Green chimed in, "seeing their growth, is one of the great joys of parenthood." She and Ben had left their son, Scott, behind at Butterfly House. He was named for their first-born son who had been killed in the Vietnam War. They also had two grown living children, and grandchildren, from their previous life on Earth. Like the rest of the Brigade, they took a wait-and-see attitude about having more children.

At first, doubts about the viability of commanders' offspring came into question when Bess and Arthur Perlman's child was stillborn. That had occurred aboard the Mothership before it reached Earth on the last mission there. This tragedy had given pause to all Brigade members, particularly the other commanders. But subsequent births had been normal; Commander Mary Green had Scott, and Chief Commander Ruth Charnofsky had Autumn. If the space travel status of the children of Butterfly House was positive, then the Greens, along with other commanders and Brigade members, planned to expand their families.

Babies and raising children was something Amos Bright preferred not to discuss. There were many methods of reproduction in the Universe. Some were quite dispassionate, like the Antareans. Others, like Earth-humanoids, were filled with sensual contact and, to Antareans, an elusive, troubling emotion called love. Although love seemed to have much to do with loyalty, an important Antarean trait, it was more than that. Quite confusing, Amos thought. And distracting. Secretly, he wondered which The Master's preferred way was. The lack of a physical reproduction process did not bother Amos Bright. However, the emotional love-making, and then love for and from a child, pulled at a place from deep inside his cloned body. Trying to comprehend this sensation exposed an inexplicable void within—a dark and empty place. The Brigade's gift for ingratiating themselves with strangers seemed to have something to do with the love characteristic. That phenomenon also piqued his curiosity, and fear that he was somehow incomplete.

"Well," Bright continued politely, as he felt compelled to answer Mary Green, "you've all observed that the drive to bear and raise young is quite different among the species of our galaxy. It is a phenomenon as varied as the number of planets." Then, before the commanders had a chance to reply, he changed the subject. "But please, dear friends, tell me what do you hear from the others?"

"The other commanders?" Art Perlman asked.

"Yes."

"They are all well and busy. The Finleys are onto something quite special, I hear."

"On Klane," Bright said, smiling. "Yes. We hope to have a message from them soon." Bright wondered if one of these commanders might have already received one. "And the children? Tell me. How are they?"

"Bernie says the kids are great!" Art answered quickly. "We can't wait to see them."

"Then you know about the mission?"

"Know about it?" Ben Green said. "Hell, Amos, we requested it!"

"I see." Amos was curious. He knew about the impending mission. The High Council had discussed it. But he had not been told where, or how, it had originated. He had assumed it was a subject still open to discussion. Now, according to these commanders, the Earth mission was approved. He wondered, in light of the communication need for a Brigade commander to be aboard the inter-galactic probes being planned, how these five commanders could all be allowed to travel to Earth.

"It's the children," Bess Perlman informed the Antarean. "They communicate that they are ready to leave their sanctuary."

"Ready to leave?" Amos was surprised. "But this is not their choice."

"Well, uh...yes. You're right," Bess said awkwardly, realizing that Amos was not informed about the children's insistence.

"Of course, they will be evaluated first," Art continued, hoping to blunt Bright's growing unease.

"But they refuse to allow that to happen without our being there," Ben Green added.

Amos Bright absorbed this new information. He also sensed that his Brigade friends were not telling him everything about events at Butterfly House. There was an awkward silence. None of the commanders wanted to stay on the subject. Amos sensed that too. They were thinking of him as an old friend, but as an Antarean High Council member as well.

"Gideon Mersky is here," Amos announced, changing the subject once again, thinking to keep the commanders off balance. He felt their surprise as they reacted and recalled how resistant the ex-Defense Secretary had been to their leaving Earth after the children were born. He had gone behind the back of President Teller, with a plan to hold them by force, a plan that had been foiled. Although Mersky finally came around to accepting the necessity for the children to depart, and he still believed they had, the Brigade commanders did not trust him. That is why he was never told that the children had remained on Earth.

"Mersky here, you say? Now what's that all about, Amos?" Ben Green asked.

"I promised him that when he came of age, if... if he wished, he could join the Brigade."

"Things have changed," Mary Green said. Amos Bright sensed rapid communication between the commanders in the room, but they blocked him from its content.

"He may even become a commander," Bright told them, stirring the pot.

"Shouldn't we have been consulted?" Art Perlman asked. His voice had an unfriendly edge to it.

"Well, yes...and you will be, if it is to happen. Perhaps it will be discussed in today's meeting. But please, dear friends, remember it was also we...I who invited you to leave Earth," Bright reminded them. The commanders were suddenly wary of Bright's heavy-handed reference.

"As a reward, I recall, for helping you out of a rather difficult situation," Ben Green told Bright.

"Yes. Of course. And we are eternally grateful to you all for helping to save our cocooned army." Bright bowed to them all. "In any event, it was I who made the promise to Mr. Mersky."

"You might have said something," Ben Green continued.

"Well...there happened to be a Shar-Bakart transport passing close to Earth. And I knew it was time to keep my promise, so I contacted Jack Fischer...you know..."

"Yes," Ruth answered for all of them. "He is sensitive to telepathy."

"I taught him, you'll recall," Amos said.

"We remember," Ben Green said, impatient to get past Bright's diplomatic tap dance.

"Of course. Well, I had Mr. Fischer approach Mr. Mersky, who immediately accepted. He was shuttled to the transport and processed. And he has adapted beautifully."

"He would," Art Perlman said sarcastically. "He was always a bit of a chameleon." The reference went beyond Bright's understanding of Earth-human sarcasm.

"I'm told he even took a...well, he was said to have spent sexual time with a Brigade member during the trip here," Bright continued. "A woman named Annabella Costa. Do you know her?"

"I know her," Mary Green answered. "I know her..."

"A very nice woman, I understand," Bright said, smiling. "A dancer of some sort?" Now Bright was exercising his own sarcasm.

"She was a stripper. Lived in Tampa, as I recall," Mary said somewhat disdainfully. "A real Southern Belle."

"Is that not honorable?" Bright asked tongue in cheek. He had heard and seen enough about Earthly mores to know what a stripper was. The commanders knew his question was disingenuous. Bright was playing them.

"It's a living," Mary Green replied. "But maybe a little, uh, tacky...By Antarean standards, that is." Her joke broke the tension in the room. They all laughed.

"Well, yes," Amos said softly with a patronizing nod. "But I do think that Mr. Mersky has the potential to command and..." Suddenly, a gentle drone, sounding like a Buddhist chant, filled the air. "Ahhhh," Bright announced, "the call to High Council. I must leave you, dear friends. Let's have a chat about this after you've all seen Mr. Mersky. I think you'll be surprised at how he's, what's the word? Oh yes, mellowed." He bowed graciously. "I will see you in council." He bowed again and left the five commanders wondering. They would now wait until the High Council called them.

"Imagine," Ben Green said, after Amos Bright closed the door to the anteroom behind him, "Gideon Mersky as one of us!"

They all understood how making Gideon Mersky a Brigade commander might serve the Antareans. The newly discovered commanders' ability to message across deep-space instantly was critical to Antarean inter-galactic exploration. This new reliance on the Brigade commanders made their hosts uneasy. That, and the strong bond that Earth-humans had built with the Parmans and other beings caused additional Antarean concern. Perhaps, unknown to the Brigade, others on Earth were being considered for commands as well?

"Mersky was a born-again zealot," Arthur Perlman said aloud, suspecting that the High Council had recording devices in the anteroom. He wanted to go on record.

"Maybe he's changed," Bess suggested. "What do you think, Mary?" Mary Green did not answer. She raised her hand for the others to clear their minds as she concentrated on a message coming from afar.

"Listen," Mary said softly, "and join with me." The others ended the discussion about Mersky and pooled their telepathic resources. "I don't think it is for us," Mary said as they connected to the message.

"You're right," Ben Green whispered. "It's from Joe Finley for Bernie Lewis." For a reason not yet known, Ben Green's message reception was better than the others, even better than that of Brigade Chief Commander Ruth Charnofsky. "He's worried about something...The children...Our Earth mission..." Their concentration was interrupted by the hiss of the door opening. An Antarean guardian, a soldier, stepped into the anteroom and summoned them to appear before the High Council.

CHAPTER FIVE
MESSAGES FROM AFAR

On Earth, 169 light years across the galaxy from Antares, a cloudless night and waning moon over Cayman Brac allowed a brilliant display in the heavens. Here, south of The Tropic of Cancer and north of the Tropic of Capricorn, the densest part of the Milky Way spreads directly above and across the night sky. Beyond this familiar spectacle were millions more galaxies, containing billions upon billions of stars, planets, moons and asteroids. The Universe was filled with life that was growing, becoming, changing and interacting. Depending on one's point of view, it could appear chaotic, haphazard or harmonious...or all three combined. But one fact was clear—all that exists in the cosmos is of a common origin; from wispy, swirling gas clouds to the hardest diamonds; all matter; all life—everything derives and is formed from stardust.

To those who have yet to travel into space and discover the living Universe, it remains a mystery. For them, the origins of life are shrouded in religious beliefs that substitute for fact.

Many who are advanced enough to probe nearby space and planets, and find no life, remain convinced they are the only intelligent creatures in the cosmos. That kind of parochial, narrow-minded conclusion tends to encourage arrogance and a sense of superiority.

Those who do travel our galaxy, or have been contacted by explorers, travelers and traders like the Antareans, know they are not alone in the Universe. From that knowledge there emerges a far deeper respect for life and its wondrous gifts. In spite of breaches of harmony that thieves, fools and despots bring to existence, most are at peace and living in harmony.

So it was on Earth this soft Caribbean night as Melody Messina and Beam Amato strolled hand in hand a few yards back from the tide's incoming surge. As they made their way down the beach, the fine, cool white sand sifting through their bare toes was a familiar and pleasant sensation. The two girls were the closest of friends. As with all the children of Butterfly House, they had known each other before their births.

Melody was tanned, tall, and quick to smile. She was the oldest of the children. Yesterday she had turned sixteen. The Erhardt twins, Joshua and Eric, the only others born in space before the Mothership had arrived on Earth, were seven minutes younger. The rest of the children, with the exception of the two youngest of the Martindale clan, would all turn sixteen during the next four months.

"My parents are there now," Beam Amato said wistfully, pointing toward three visible pinpoints of light—a grouping that Earth-humans called Andromeda. Two were stars: one a Red Giant, the other a Blue Dwarf. The third pinpoint was a galaxy more than 400 light years beyond. "Near Red-1104-Quad 7 on Klane." Beam, a highly sensitive young lady who possessed fine artistic talents, was quieter than most of the children. But when they gathered as a group, she served as one of the focal points through which the children channeled their burgeoning powers, especially when thoughts or ideas needed to be visualized.

"They're with the Sloor! That's so cool," Melody responded.

"It's time for the emergence," Beam continued. All the children knew about the Brigade mission to Klane. Something extraordinary was happening to the Sloor—an evolutionary leap. The children's ability to possess such knowledge was their secret, one of many they now kept from their guardians and teachers.

The girls paused and sat down on the sand. They both laid back and scanned the heavens. Melody's gaze settled on the constellation Scorpio and the star Antares' system. Like Earth, only Antares cradled humanoid life—an ice planet whose inhabitants live ten miles below the surface, deriving energy and sustenance from their planet's molten core.

"My parents are on Antares," Melody said softly as she pointed toward the familiar constellation. "For the gathering."

"They're so lucky," Beam said. "Mine will have to wait five more years for the next gathering to see their old friends."

"They're doing very important work."

"Yes," she said wistfully. "Anyway, I'm sure we'll meet up with them when we..." Her words were interrupted by a high-pitched greeting song from a pod of gray whales passing south of Cuba. Both young women telepathed back a greeting of peace and safe journey. Then, before they could resume their conversation, another message from much farther away captured their attention.

For most of the night, Melody and Beam sat silently on the cool sand beneath the canopy of stars. The tide crept up to and over their toes, but not beyond. Silvery tarpon chased small schools of anchovies in the surf. But the girls were oblivious to their surroundings as they received a detailed message from Brigade Chief Commander Ruth Charnofsky, also now on Antares for the gathering. The communication stated that most of the Brigade parents of children at Butterfly House were now on Antares. There were also special instructions for their guardians and teachers. As dawn approached, the two girls felt another message directed toward Brigade Commander Bernie Lewis, their guardian on Earth. It was from Joe Finley on Klane.

Morning announced its arrival with a purple-to-blue-to-pink glow in the East. When the sun appeared on the horizon, Melody and Beam, excited and enthused by the information they now possessed, rose, brushed off the sand from their legs and clothes, and walked quickly toward the steep path that wound its way up the cliff to Butterfly House.

The hotel's white stucco walls, bathed in morning's first light, glowed with a bright golden-orange hue. As they climbed upward, both girls sensed the other children were awake and excited. They quickened their pace. Butterfly House was going to have special visitors. There was much for everyone to do. A landing party from Antares would soon be on the way!

By the time they reached the gatehouse and cleared the alarm system, a tropical Reuben's sky, baby-blue with puffy white clouds, foretold of another beautiful island day ahead. Melody and Beam joined the rest of Butterfly House's inhabitants for breakfast on the main mansion's east terrace. Like the two girls, the other twenty-four Earth-human children, and Laga Martindale, appeared much older than their sixteen Earth-years.

Laga was a six-foot six-inch giant—a beautiful mixture of his father's Earth-humanoid processed genes and his mother's Penditan heritage. The two other Martindale children, a boy, Lucas, and a girl, Rode, were eight and three years old respectively. They, too, were tall for their ages and possessed powerful and sturdy bodies. Like their mother, their skin was Penditan bronze in tone. But they had Peter Martindale's finer Caucasian features and steel-blue eyes.

The Penditan are a tall, dark, and muscular tribal humanoid race. Their society is matriarchal. Males and females partake equally in the hunt. Life centers on family and tribe, intertwined with abiding respect for their natural place in the ecology of their planet. Like many humanoids that do not space-travel, the belief in their origin is shrouded in folklore and mystery. But their appearance and genetic makeup, similar to all humanoids, bears out the supposition of a universal common ancestry—a seed scattered throughout the galaxy eons ago.

There are countless planets, many of them originally lifeless, that have been colonized by various space explorers seeking minerals, gases, exotic liquids, precious stones, chemicals, energy sources and fuels. Many of these barren outposts are low-gravity moons and asteroids whose cratered surfaces are comprised of jagged rocks, ferrite and a host of other minerals and cosmic dust. They have no natural food sources. Most are devoid of moisture, though some of the mineral deposits do contain ice crystals.

The developers, explorers, miners and wildcatters who work these places prize the animal meat of Turmoline, for its taste and high nutritional content. The furs and skins of Amaracks and Finogels, two of the planet's animals hunted by the Penditan, are famous for their warmth and durability, a necessity on many of these forbidding outposts.

Tern and Peter Martindale met at Turmoline's annual market. It takes place in the dry season, on a delta at the confluence of three great rivers where the forty-six Turmoline tribes bring their wares to trade with space merchants, travelers and each other. Over the millennia, the Penditan tribe developed a particularly lucrative trade of furs, skins, and smoked protein-rich meats with the most successful space merchants, the Antareans.

Tern had learned to operate the Antarean universal language translator, which now contained English. She was assigned to escort Peter Martindale for the market's duration. At that same time there were sexual stirrings in Peter Martindale, a direct consequence of the deep-space processing the Brigade had received before they left Earth. Although he did not understand these long-dead emotions upwelling in him, he knew he was strongly attracted to Tern. He followed his romantic instincts. In Earth terms, Tern was more than fifty years younger than Peter. But she responded to his advances and they fell in love. He asked her to marry him.

Custom among the Penditan is that a marriage request could only be considered after a year of service to the tribe—a time equivalent to nearly two Earth-years. Smitten, Peter Martindale was eager to accept the terms. But he needed permission to stay on Turmoline from Brigade Chief Commander Ruth Charnofsky, and his Antarean Mothership Commander.

Martindale's Antarean commander did not like the idea of losing a crew member. On the other hand, Brigade Chief Commander Ruth Charnofsky, married to Panatoy, a Subaxian from the planet Rigel, was sympathetic to mixed-mating. She had a beautiful daughter, Autumn, to prove it.

"Do you love this girl?" Ruth asked when she met privately with Peter Martindale.

"I surely do," he answered immediately and with conviction. "I feel like a schoolboy on his first date, Ruth. My heart races when I see her. I only want to be near her. Is that crazy for a seventy-nine year old man?" Because she was in contact with the other commanders, Ruth was aware that this kind of behavior was now becoming common among Brigade members, and toward many other humanoids the Brigade encountered in their travels and work.

"Then stay here and love her," Ruth told Peter Martindale. "I'll handle the Antareans." And she did. Now Tern and Peter Martindale, and their three children, lived on Earth in Butterfly House.

The adults usually ate breakfast together at a separate table on the patio, meeting to discuss the day's schedule. This morning they arrived after the children. Alicia Sanchez Margolin, who had earned her MS in Astrophysics at MIT, and her PhD in Quantum Mechanics at Stanford, strolled onto the terrace first. She was tall and slender, with sparkling dark brown eyes and long, thick, black hair that cascaded and curled onto her broad, athletic shoulders. She was gracefully approaching her forty-third birthday. Her voice was always soft and calming, her manner self-assured.

Most of the communication between the children, Alicia, and her husband Philip, was telepathic. Prior to their birth, these children were aware of the world they were about to enter. They had collectively chosen Alicia and Philip to be their guardians. In fact, the children had miraculously taught telepathy to Alicia and Philip from the womb, a function that only required an expansion of a mere four percent of human brain capability.

Bernie and Rose Lewis arrived at breakfast shortly after Alicia. They always greeted the children with a resounding, "Good morning, everyone!" They were answered in unison.

"Good morning, Aunt Rose! Good morning, Uncle Bernie!" The greeting sounded like a troop of summer campers greeting their head counselor at morning roll call.

"Yes. Yes. It is a good morning, isn't it?" Commander Bernie Lewis shouted back, waving his arms and smiling. "A beautiful morning." He glanced over at Melody and Beam who had joined the Erhardt twins for breakfast. "I was up early this morning," he called to Melody. "I heard the good news myself."

"What news?" Alicia Margolin asked.

"We're to have visitors!" Melody Messina shouted excitedly. Everyone cheered. At that moment, Philip Margolin stepped onto the patio. Holding up his hands and waving, he played to the cheers like an Academy Award winner.

"Thank you. Thank you, one and all. I know I'm your favorite teacher and guardian, but in all modesty, I'd like to thank all the little people who..."

"It's not for you, Mr. Popular," Alicia interrupted. "We're going to have visitors!"

"What visitors?" Phil queried, as he joined his wife at the table with the Lewises. Philip was shorter than Alicia, and two years younger. His stocky, five-foot, nine-inch frame rested on powerful, muscular legs that he kept finely tuned with a five mile run on the beach every day. His areas of expertise were computer science and chemistry—specifically propulsion. He too held MS and Ph.D. degrees.

Before the children arrived, Alicia and Philip had been working for NASA, and the Department of Defense, on top-secret projects. They had been brought in as consultants by then Secretary of State Gideon Mersky when the Antareans last visited Earth. It was their planning that enabled an Antarean Watership, a huge transport that brought that life sustaining fluid to distant Antarean outposts, to land undetected near the American East Coast to safely deliver the pregnant Brigade members, their husbands and mates. After the children were born, and the decision was made to leave them behind on Earth until it was safe for them to travel in space, Alicia and Philip were formally installed as teachers and guardians. By then, they had fallen in love. They married and had a son, Michael, now six, and Carmella, a daughter not quite six months old.

"Visitors from where?" Philip asked again, as he sat down.

"Antares," Bernie Lewis told him. "They sent a message last night. A Mothership is..."

"A Mothership! Is it the whole Brigade?" Philip asked excitedly.

Carmella Margolin chose that moment to squeal a delightful "Daddy!" from her high chair. She offered her father her plastic orange juice bottle. Although Carmella uttered her first word at three months, the children of Butterfly House had begun to communicate with her while she was still in Alicia's womb. The language they used was one they remembered from their own gestational period. It was, they now knew, a universal telepathed language common to all cerebrally communicative species prior to birth. Even though they were not offspring of Geriatric Brigade parents, Michael and Carmella Margolin were developing mentally at a fantastic rate. Their parents suspected this was due to their contact with the children of Butterfly House. The children knew it was true.

"Good morning, Sweetheart," Philip said lovingly to his daughter.

"Do you want some juice, Daddy?" the baby offered again. Philip was anxious to hear about the visitors. A quick telepathic message from Bernie told him that they would discuss the details later. Philip accepted the juice from his daughter, who then offered him a wobbly spoonful of her cereal. Rose Lewis laughed with delight.

"Carmella, my sweet, you'll be running this place before you're two," Rose Lewis said as she bent over and kissed the precocious child on the forehead.

"Thank you, Aunt Rose," the baby answered. She then pulled the spoon away from her father and presented it to Rose Lewis. "Want some?"

"No thank you, Dear. I'll stick with fruit today." Rose helped herself to a banana and a ripe mango from a fruit bowl in the center of the table. Bernie, her husband of sixty-seven years, reached over and took the fruit from her.

"I'll peel those for you, m'darlin'," he said, taking care of her the way he had for most of their lives, including the past sixteen years as the children's protectors. Bernie was a Brigade commander. Rose chose not to take on that responsibility. In fact, when Amos Bright had originally made the offer to bring the 941 Earth-human seniors into space, Rose Lewis had been a holdout. She was not sure that leaving Earth for an uncertain future, even though it promised a much longer and more useful life, was the right thing to do. But she relented when Bernie, who wanted to go very much, told her that he would stay behind.

"Without you, my love," Bernie told Rose, "a long and adventurous life would be nothing." Rose was the last to make the decision to go. That was twenty-one years ago. Five years after that, at the end of the return trip to Earth, staying behind with the children was a decision that Rose and Bernie willingly made together. It was Bernie Lewis who had convinced the other nine Brigade commanders, and Amos Bright, that it was necessary to have one commander stay behind, to guard and help educate the children. He also argued that Rose and he could serve as a study of the effects of being processed and remaining on Earth.

Bernie was a World War II veteran, a P-51 pilot in the Pacific. He learned to fly the Antarean Probeship that was used to bring the babies, the Martindales, and the Lewises back to Earth after a faked departure. The Probeship, a sleek spacecraft capable of incredible sub-light speed, was now hidden thirty feet under the sea, beneath the outcropping of a nearby coral reef.

"If the children are not able to travel until they are old, their parents will want to visit with them," Bernie suggested. "Will the Antarean deep-space travel processing that reversed their aging remain intact? Or, once on Earth for a period of time, might their rejuvenated bodies and expanded mental capacities revert back to more Earthly aging processes?"

So far, the news was good. Bernie's and Rose's physical condition stabilized equivalently to the age of thirty-five. Their enhanced mental capacities were not diminished. They were energetic, and their altered immune systems kept them disease-free. The Lewises had not conceived a child in space, but were well aware of the return to fertility experienced by them and all the other members of the Brigade. Rose ovulated every twenty-eight days. She was capable of 83% brain function. Bernie, because of his enhancement to commander, was capable of 90%. The children's brain usage and capacity had reached those limits, and perhaps beyond, but how much beyond? Would the children age in the normal definition of human experience? It appeared they had evolved beyond what anyone Earth-human, Brigade or Antarean, had anticipated. Would that make them eligible for deep-space travel now? And if so, would they want to go?

These were perplexing questions. They remained unanswered because, for the past three years, the children refused medical and intellectual examinations, making their prospect of leaving Earth problematic. How they would respond to the visitors sent to evaluate their ability for deep-space travel was also unknown.

CHAPTER SIX
THE SLOOR EMERGE

One moment, the surface of the gray, oily sea was calm and the next, it was alive with Sloor. They had emerged from the depths twenty Klanian days ahead of schedule. And there were twice as many as the last emergence. The adults, who were juveniles then and had presented great evolutionary changes, now appeared to have had an even more radical metamorphosis. They were much larger than their parents had been. Their once dull-brown, scaly outer skin was now a smooth, iridescent green and lavender. Sprouting from it, along their backs and shoulders, were long, shiny black feathers.

The Sloor young were everywhere—in far greater numbers than that last emergence. They, too, were very different. In the prior emergence, the babies had been lethargic and disoriented, clinging to the adults as they broke the surface of the ocean. But this time they were active and aggressive, playing with one another, emitting high-pitched sounds of gleeful excitement.

As more of the Sloor swam to shore and stepped onto land, they spread their wings to allow the warm Klanian sun to dry them. They looked like huge cormorants. The larger adult males displayed magnificent multi-colored wings, framing their bodies like blazing rainbows. There was audible contact between them and the smaller females who also dried their coal-black wings in the sun. They had a language—something they had not revealed before. A startling part of their metamorphosis was that while the adults were air breathing and still retained gills, the young were breathing the Klanian atmosphere directly through air holes that had replaced gills.

Joe and Alma Finley, joined by Paul and Marie Amato, and three "Ants," set up an observation post well back from the shoreline. One of Joe Finley's duties was to notify the Antarean High Council of the emergence via the Brigade commanders physically closest to the council. That would be Ruth Charnofsky, now on Antares for the gathering. But Finley was moved by a force he didn't quite understand to direct the message toward Commander Bernie Lewis, on Earth. As he sent it, he knew that the commanders on Antares would also receive the message and would understand the need to keep the communiqué secret.

"The Sloor have emerged," he began. "They have changed radically. They are larger. They have developed audible language. We are now observing from a distance but will try to contact them directly. Since this emergence was not anticipated to happen so soon, no council member is present. Commander Beam has assumed the mantle of Ambassador. We expect her on site momentarily. What we have observed is an unprecedented evolutionary event—a quantum leap. The Sloor have metamorphosed beyond the amphibian stage. The young are air breathing and without gills. The adults are now feathered and very tall—over thirty feet tall. This is fantastic! Bernie, these advances are stunning."

As Joe Finley watched the Sloor continue to emerge and gather on land, spreading their wings to dry, a thought entered his consciousness.

"Do not inform the Antarean High Council about our emergence. You must wait until we meet your children!" Then he realized it was not a thought, but a distinct voice. Joe felt his wife's hand on his arm.

"It's the Sloor," Alma Finley told her husband. "They are contacting us telepathically!" She had received the same message. "But how can they know about the children and the council?"

"I don't know," Joe answered. Then the disembodied voice returned.

"We know your children. They have been teaching us for two cycles now. They have cautioned us to speak to only you, and to block the others you travel with."

"How can this be?" Alma asked, telepathically. "How did they teach you?"

"They have visited us. They have visited many, in fact."

"Many? Many Sloor?" Joe asked.

"Many beings. Many species," was the incredible answer. The voice was warm and comforting, much in the same tone that their children used when they sent loving messages to their parents. "That's why the revelation this Sloor made about the children visiting Klane and other places sounded so credible," Joe thought to himself. But how was direct contact possible? The children had never left Earth. Or had they? With the exception of the Martindale kids, Joe knew all the children had been away from Cayman Brac for three years, ostensibly traveling around Earth for their education. But that didn't explain how they could know the Sloor.

A large adult, whose wings had dried, made his way toward the observers.

"One of them is coming," Marie Amato pointed out. At that same moment, the Antarean commander, Beam, arrived on the scene. She wore the flowing red and black robe of an Antarean Ambassador over her protective clothing. She stepped forward to greet the large Sloor adult. He was a giant, towering over the seven foot Beam by twenty-five feet. His wings, now folded, settled neatly along his curved, protruding spinal column.

"We are arrived," the Sloor said telepathically, to all the visitors present. The voice was a deep, deliberate base. Beam lifted her arms above her head, palms up, fingers apart and pointed outward—a sign of greeting and non-aggression. The towering Sloor bowed slightly and spread his wondrously colored wings. Fully extended, their span was over fifty feet. The feathers were more metallic than silken. They glittered like shimmering points of multi-tinted fire in the red, Klanian daylight.

"You are welcome to our home," the Sloor announced. He gently folded his wings.

"On behalf of the Antarean High Council," Beam responded, "I thank you for your welcome. On behalf of all Antareans, I greet you as their Ambassador. These, my companions, are from the planet Earth. We ask permission to remain on your planet to communicate with you."

"To what purpose?" the Sloor giant asked. Beam then solemnly uttered the ancient Antarean first-greeting, as it has been delivered innumerable times on newly discovered planets, to all newly discovered races, species and life forms.

"To develop a bond of friendship. To share our knowledge of the Universe, and all that we have discovered. To invite you to share with us, and other beings of peace, the bounty of The Master's creation."

"Yes. I understand," the Sloor announced. "You may stay for now."

"Thank you," Beam answered.

"You are welcome until we are all arrived and mated. Then we will meet again and see to your needs. You may observe in silence." He turned abruptly toward the sea and, as he did, he spread his great wings, flapped them twice and, with a rush of air, rose majestically and rapidly into the bright-red, cloudless Klanian sky.

His assent was a signal to the others. Hundreds of winged adults, males and females, rose into the sky with him. To Joe Finley, who had been an avid fly fisherman on Earth, the ascending Sloor appeared like a hatch of giant insects that had emerged from underwater and were rising in their mating flight.

"Are your recording this?" Beam asked Joe Finley.

"Of course. From the moment they emerged, Ambassador Beam."

CHAPTER SEVEN
THE CHILDREN'S JOURNEY

The Lewises had a great deal of planning to do for the visit. First on the agenda was to test the Probeship's electronic and guidance systems and fire up the engines. The ship had not been flown for more than a year. It would be needed to shuttle visitors from wherever the Antarean Mothership parked, should the commander of the vessel decide that an Earth landing was risky. And there was always the possibility of an emergency evacuation. The Probeship had to be ready to work as a submersible as well as an aircraft. Every contingency had to be anticipated. Should alien visitors be discovered, the media frenzy would quickly grow into a circus and become overwhelming to the visitors and their mission.

Although Bernie Lewis was the Probeship's pilot, he had also trained Rose to operate it. Twice in the past five years they had taken the diminutive spacecraft to the moon and back. On the last trip, Rose navigated and piloted both ways, proving her proficiency.

In spite of the news of the impending visit, Alicia and Phil Margolin decided to follow the children's daily schedule. After breakfast, the children cleaned their rooms, then gathered for their daily exercise session, to be led by Laga Martindale, As always, it would be rigorous. Laga was a physical fitness devotee. At six-foot five-inches, and two-hundred thirty-six pounds, Laga was a robust Penditan specimen. Since the children's recent return from the outside world, Laga had taken upon himself to keep everyone in top physical condition. His motivation was not altogether altruistic. Long ago, his parents had decided that when feasible, they would bring their children to live on Turmoline, with their Penditan tribe.

To that end, Laga's mother, Tern, made sure her children would be ready to take their place among her tribe's hunters. She schooled Laga in her tribal ways and in the use of Penditan weapons—the Sharr—a large and powerful crossbow; the Banetto—a throwing club that resembled a boomerang; and the awesome Kalkacho—a fifteen-inch, double-bladed Penditan hunting knife made of metals mined, fired, alloyed and forged on Turmoline. Laga's younger brother, Lucas, was almost old enough to begin his lessons. Their younger sister, Rode, would have to wait a few more years.

When the warm-up was finished, Laga announced the morning's four-part program to the children.

"We will begin with a mile swim—six times back and forth across horseshoe cove." The day was going to be a hot one and the children cheered at the thought of a cool swim. Laga, serious as ever, continued, "Then we will scale the cliffs below Butterfly House. Teams of two. Full equipment." A few of the children groaned. "At the top of the cliff we will gather for fifteen minutes of Sento." This was the Penditan version of Tai-chi. "And we will end today's session with a two-mile run around the perimeter of Cayman Brac's magnificent airport," Laga said wryly. It was a tiny field with a dirt runway and a one-room, one-story stucco building that served as a terminal, taxi station and ticket counter. There were two planes that flew from Grand Cayman to Little Cayman, to Cayman Brac, and back.

As the Lewises prepared to inspect the Probeship, Bernie sensed the incoming message from Joe Finley. While developing the confidence to use the new form of communication, he was still uncertain as to its accuracy. One thing he knew. Reception required his complete concentration.

"I need to clear my mind," he told Rose. She was not a commander, but understood what he meant, and went off to visit a tidy vegetable garden that she tended in a clearing on the southeast side of Butterfly House. Bernie hurried down to the dock and boarded the "Razzamatazz," a forty-foot Ocean Yacht that belonged to Phil Doyle. Phil was an old and trusted friend of Jack Fischer and the Brigade.

He was visiting Butterfly House from his home on Isla Morada, in the Florida Keys.

As Bernie settled down in the fighting chair, bolted firmly to the teak aft deck, he observed the children completing their swim. All twenty-two were there, led by the imposing figure of the bronze giant, Laga. "How far they have come," Bernie Lewis mused aloud. His chest swelled with pride, knowing that Rose and he had fulfilled their promise to the children's parents, keeping their charges safe and undetected. The children emerged from the azure water—strong and self-assured, and, he suspected, ready to strike out on their own. But whatever plans they had, they had kept secret.

The message from Joe Finley on Klane questioned something about the children that Bernie did not totally grasp. But he knew that whatever was being sent would be implanted in that part of his genetic makeup that they, the Brigade commanders, now called their "library." The message's detailed contents would be stored, like email waiting to be retrieved, opened and read carefully. He could determine the sense of the message, which portended a change in the evolutionary order of things on Klane. And Finley suspected a link to the children. But that was impossible unless...Was it possible that the children were able to communicate with non-humanoid beings across the galaxy? How? And if so, why had they kept that a secret too?

As Bernie absorbed Joe's message, the children assaulted the steep cliffs below Butterfly House in teams of two. He watched their lithe, sinewy bodies, linked by state-of-the-art mountaineering hardware, move up and among the steep, slippery facade like a herd of big horn sheep might maneuver along a Rocky Mountain ridge. Yes, he thought, they were certainly developed far beyond their sixteen years.

Bernie's mind raced back through the years that Rose and he had spent at Butterfly House. The Brigade had communicated many of their experiences back to the Lewises and the children, but nothing could substitute for actually being out there in deep-space. Yet Rose and Bernie had no regrets.

The early years had been the most stressful, when the children were infants requiring constant nurturing, love and attention. The absence of the children's real parents had worried Rose and Bernie. Could they be an acceptable substitute for so many? Through the years, as Antarean Motherships carried Brigade parents far from their offspring, messages of love and caring were sent back and forth from parent to child. That had eased the Lewises burdens somewhat.

Bernie sat in the fighting chair watching the children climb. "You guys say you're ready to leave," he said aloud. "Well, so are we." He and Rose had not aged. In fact, they felt and looked much younger than when they had first settled in on Cayman Brac. "We've done well," he thought. The secret of Butterfly House was secure. The Margolins had fulfilled their education responsibility brilliantly, although at times it was difficult to distinguish the pupils from the teachers. The physical trainers, Peter and Tern Martindale, and now Laga, had kept the children on an excellent diet and exercise plan from day one. If the approaching visit was to ascertain their ability to travel in deep-space, Bernie was now certain they had the strength and endurance necessary to pass the test.

And Jack Fischer, Phil Doyle and Mad Man Mazuski, the only Earth-humans who knew about the children, had performed their functions superbly as contacts and conduits of earthly information and supplies, as had Mr. DePalmer, their secretive Miami banker.

Within the secure boundaries of the compound, the children had flourished. Their extraordinary immune systems kept them disease-free. At the age of two years, seven months, their formal education began. But in fact, they had been absorbing knowledge since before they were born. By six, they had collectively reached the equivalent of ninth grade. By ten, they were high school graduates. By twelve, they had completed undergraduate work in Liberal Arts, Science, History, Astronomy, Biology and Political Science. All the time, they were communicated information about the galaxy from their parents and Brigade commanders. On occasion, they heard from Antarean commanders Amos Bright and Beam, although that had recently ended. Then Bernie recalled, with some trepidation, that in their thirteenth year, all of the children, except Laga, announced that they wanted to leave the island and expand their horizons. They said there was nothing more for them to learn on Cayman Brac. They wanted to explore their home planet and meet its inhabitants in person. At that point, Bernie and Rose Lewis, like most parents, knew they had to let go.

Forged high school and college transcripts were prepared through Jack Fischer. Applications were sent out to colleges, universities and businesses around the world. The children were accepted wherever they applied. For nearly three years, they had roamed the Earth, first singly, and then in twos and threes.

Some attended school, garnering their Master's and Doctorate degrees. Others worked in business, on farms and even labored in factories. They traveled with the Bedouin; read law at Harvard; mined diamonds in South Africa; studied medicine at the Sorbonne; herded sheep in the Australian outback; taught Spanish to Russian children in Siberia; programmed super-computers in Silicon Valley; helped design hydro-electric projects in China; fed the hungry in Ethiopia and Sudan; studied the destruction of rain forests in Brazil and Malaysia; tracked El Niño from Polynesia to Texas; and confirmed the potential devastation that greenhouse gases posed to life on Earth. Their activities involved every continent, most cultures, and many languages.

They stayed away from the political, ethnic and racial conflicts that plagued humanity, as the twenty-first century began. With their powers they knew they could influence human minds. Although they had left the island to explore the world as individuals, what one learned, all learned; what one experienced, all experienced; what one sensed, all sensed. They studied, observed and pondered Earth's problems, potentials and future. But they chose not to interfere. At least not yet. At least not directly.

Eight months ago, they began to return, one at a time and unannounced. They had grown, physically and in wisdom far beyond their nearly sixteen years. They had matured to a level of intellect previously unknown in children of any age. Something profound had occurred. Before they traveled, individually the children had superior intellect. In twos and threes, their capacities increased tenfold. But now, because they all refused to be tested, their teachers and guardians could not say how much their knowledge and power had increased, especially when all twenty-two focused in concert. Laga, who had not gone on the journey with his peers, was silent on the matter. Bernie sensed the children's abilities were far beyond anything a Brigade commander possessed, or for that matter, the power of the ten commanders combined.

The Lewises withheld their opinions about the changes in the children. They would wait and watch until they knew what it meant. But now, with the apparent news that the Sloor on Klane had somehow been contacted and were communicating with the children, Bernie confided to Rose that he was relieved about the mission from Antares.

"The kids know what they must do," Bernie told his wife. "My bones tell me they have a special mission of their own."

CHAPTER EIGHT
THE HIGH COUNCIL

While the Brigade enjoyed their reunion, the five commanders were respectfully guided to their seats facing the fifteen Antarean High Council members, and the council leader, Spooner. The atmosphere was charged. Ruth Charnofsky sensed that the meeting would be difficult. The Antareans were keenly interested in the disposition of the children. Some, including Amos Bright, questioned the wisdom of making the trip to Earth at this time.

Spooner, ever the diplomat, began by welcoming Brigade Chief Commander Ruth Charnofsky, then the Perlmans and Greens, thanking each for their service. She pointed out that at that very moment, Brigade Commanders Joe and Alma Finley were on Klane on an important mission; Bernie Lewis was serving on Earth at Butterfly House; and Brigade Commanders Hank Hankinson and Betty Franklin were about to initiate inter-galactic travel.

"You are all doing great service to The Master's Grand Plan. We are all very proud of the Geriatric Brigade," Spooner said. The rest of the council members applauded politely, using the Earth-human custom of clapping their long, tapered hands together. Because their flesh was so hard, the sound they made was like knocking two pieces of wood together. It sounded like claves used in Latin percussion. After the members had settled, Amos Bright rose from his place at the long council table. He looked down at the Brigade Commanders seated before and below him.

"We know that Earth-humanoids must live at least sixty of your years before processing is effective," Amos Bright began. "The data shows that their muscle, bone and organ structures cannot accept the rigors of processing sooner. It is safe to assume that the children are far too young to travel at their tender age." His tone was reasonable; his argument, based on fact, was reasonable. Several on the council showed their agreement with a slight nod in Bright's direction. Spooner did not. She just smiled and kept her gaze on Ruth Charnofsky.

"Are you proposing that it is dangerous for the children to be processed, Counsel Bright?" Spooner asked.

"Yes," Bright answered directly. "It is possible that even the testing might cause them physical damage."

"Thank you, Counsel Bright," Spooner said. "Commander Charnofsky, please tell us more about the children. Tell us why you must go to them now. They have only sixteen Earth-years. Surely, you must fear, as Counsel Bright says, they are too young to process."

Ruth measured her response carefully. Spooner had told her privately that the trip to Earth was approved, and that a new Mothership and crew was being readied. Had she now changed her mind? Had she been lying? Was she just appeasing Bright for the moment? Or was there some other intrigue at work here?

"It is sixteen years past their birth, Head Counsel Spooner. The children say they are ready." Ruth stood up. "Commander Lewis agrees. We are confident that your excellent medical team will be able to assess their status without putting them at risk." A few of the council members nodded with pride, but most remained stoic and uncommitted. "And as you know," Ruth continued, "the children have requested their parents, and all Brigade commanders now on Antares, be present." Several council members were visibly disturbed by Ruth's remarks. Two rose to speak, but Spooner stared them into silence.

"Children can sometimes be impatient, Commander Charnofsky," Spooner said. Her tone was condescending. There was a muttering of agreement from many on the council. "We train our young to respect the opinions and decisions of their elders." Spooner paused. "Perhaps you have been too...uh...What is that word, Counsel Bright?"

"Permissive," Bright responded softly. "And indulgent," he quickly added.

"Yes," Spooner said. "Without restrictions or parameters. No way to train the young, is it, Commanders?" She addressed them all. Ben Green was anxious to answer. Mary and he were intent on seeing their son, Scott, and were not going to tolerate a change of mind about the trip.

"That is how we choose to, as you say, train them, Head Counsel Spooner," Ben said, as he stood up. "They are, after all, Earth-humanoid, not Antarean." His tone was confrontational. Tension in the chamber escalated.

"Of course," Spooner answered calmly. "But we feel a great responsibility for them. They are, as you well know," she said with a patronizing tone, "a direct result of our invitation to you commanders, to your whole Brigade, to join us in space. This was surely part of The Master's plan."

"And we are eternally grateful," Bess Perlman said, as she now stood and addressed the council. Bess, among all the Brigade commanders, was the most diplomatic. It was an area in which she excelled on missions—a talent valued by the Antareans. "But the very existence of the 'Birth on mother's home-planet' rule signifies respect for the overwhelmingly universal bond of parent and child. And please understand that I am not criticizing how you have chosen to conceive and raise your young. We do it differently. Can that be respected?"

"Of course," Amos Bright replied. "And yet, as Head Counsel Spooner states, we feel a very strong sense of responsibility. We think of ourselves as the surrogate parents of these children."

"There is no doubt you played a major part in their, shall we say, entrance into all our lives," Ruth said. "But we, like you, believe it was the will of God, of The Master and the great universal plan that He has for us all." Her reference to The Master caused the most religious council members to nod their approval. Ruth gathered strength from their affirmation. "We believe The Master has chosen this as our time to travel among the stars and galaxies beyond. As Counsel Bright has reminded us many times—we are all only His instruments."

Earlier in Antarean evolution, a Society of Holy Ones, what Earth-humans would call priests, gained control of the governmental processes and institutions on the ice planet, much like the Popes had in Europe in the fifteenth and sixteenth centuries and as the Mullahs in Muslim countries on Earth had in the late twentieth century. It was at a time when Antareans lived closer to the surface. Up to that point, their survival had been based on genetically manipulating their race into a more cold-blooded species. The Holy Ones' religious dogma stated that The Master found these practices an abomination. They advocated cessation of genetic manipulation and a return to the ways of the past. But that would shorten life spans and decrease the population. A period of three years of debate and political unrest between the fanatical religious Holy Ones and the secular, scientifically oriented Antareans was followed by violence—a religious war that, in the end, attained nothing more than destruction and chaos. As happens in all societies that wish to survive and flourish, the radicals and religious zealots were subdued or eliminated. Negotiation and compromise eventually prevailed. Introspection became the watchword.

As inward contemplation brought peace, the Antareans sought their physical survival from within, as well. They moved deeper underground, further from the frozen wasteland of the surface, closer to the warmer core of their planet. They tapped Antares enormous geothermal energy and expanded their scientific horizons. They co-mingled religion with purpose as they developed the ability to travel in space, maintaining it was the will of The Master. They proclaimed they were a chosen race whose mission was to carry word of the Grand Plan throughout the Universe, to all life.

"But of course, Commander Charnofsky," Spooner said softly. "We are all only here to serve the Master's will."

"And as such," Amos Bright continued, "we must have the best interests of the children in mind. They, too, are His work, are they not?"

"We are grateful for your concern, Counsel Bright," Art Perlman said, as he now stood up next to his wife. "Notwithstanding medical evidence to the contrary, we too accept their presence as a gift from God. But the children say they are ready to leave Earth. Our sacred promise to them was to return when it was time for them to join with their parents in space. The children say that time is now." His manner was respectful but firm. He took his wife's arm, as a few of the council members frowned, showing their displeasure.

Spooner did not want this meeting to become mired in religious interpretation. The Antarean perception of The Master, and Earth-humans' perception of God, were not totally interchangeable. The concept that Antareans were The Master's instruments was a primary proclamation made overtly in their contacts with other beings. But respect for the beliefs of others was a primary prerequisite for all successful space travelers and traders. Head Counsel Spooner referred to some documents in front of her. She shuffled them with her long, agile, tapered fingers.

"We have the emergence of the Sloor to consider." The five Brigade commanders were surprised at the sudden change of subject. "That event is due in a short time. In her last communiqué, Commander Beam requested a council member be dispatched to Klane as Ambassador. We will require a Brigade commander on the mission as communicator."

Ruth now understood Spooner's concern. All the available Brigade commanders were scheduled to go on the Earth trip. That meant there would be no commander left on Antares for the trip to Klane, and no commander remaining on Antares to receive messages. They would have to rely on Antarean intergalactic communications—a system that took time.

"Joe and Alma Finley are on Klane," Bess Perlman suggested.

"Communication will be necessary during the trip," Bright responded quickly.

"We are stretched so thin," Ruth told Spooner. "There are only ten of us—all that was required when we replaced your cocooned army. Had we known our services would be in such demand, we would have volunteered more of us to become commanders. But now, well frankly, I don't know if any more of the Brigade are willing to undergo that change. They have their work; their plans; their lives. Many have mates and are anxious to know about the children so that they might start families of their own." Ruth's words left no doubt that she and the other commanders understood their importance to the Antareans and their maintaining their position in inter-galactic travel and trade.

"Gideon Mersky is willing to become a commander," Amos Bright announced.

"We have our doubts that Mr. Mersky is commander material," Ruth responded firmly. "However, we are open-minded and willing to explore his conversion." She turned back to Spooner. "But that will have to wait until he has adjusted to processing and his newly acquired powers. We all remember that it took some of us longer than others to accept our new physical and mental prowess.

"If we are to send an Ambassador to Klane, and all Brigade commanders are unavailable, Mr. Mersky's conversion may uh, well, it may have to be expedited," Bright suggested. Spooner and four other council members nodded affirmatively. Ruth Charnofsky was about to dispute the point, but Art Perlman spoke out with a solution.

"I will go to Klane," he stated flatly.

"And I will remain here to receive," Bess Perlman added as she took her husband's hand. "As anxious as we are to see the children, we have no child of our own at Butterfly House."

"But I understood the children wanted all of you there," Bright said. He was not happy with this turn of events. He wanted Mersky processed to commander.

"That may be true," Art Perlman said, "but as Head Counsel Spooner so aptly pointed out, there is no need to be too indulgent. I'm certain the children will understand."

"Excellent," Spooner said. Amos Bright knew Mersky's conversion to Brigade commander would have to wait.

"If that is settled, may I suggest you get your Ambassador to Klane immediately? The Sloor have already emerged," Ben Green abruptly announced. The Antarean High Council was stunned. "We had a message a moment before you called us into this meeting. The full text is not yet complete, but I can confirm that they are communicating. Commander Beam urgently requests a council member's presence." Ben decided not to elaborate on Joe Finley's transmission to Bernie Lewis. And he most certainly did not want to reveal the children's involvement with the Sloor.

"Already emerged? Most interesting. Thank you, Commander Green. When you have deciphered the message completely, please bring it to me personally," Spooner requested.

"Of course, Head Counsel Spooner. Without delay," Ben bowed respectfully.

"Then we are agreed," Spooner said with finality. "The Earth mission will go forward. The children will be tested." She turned to Ben Green. "And a message will be sent to Commander Beam, informing her that an Ambassador will depart for Klane as soon as a Mothership can be readied."

"Consider it done," Ben Green told her, bowing again. Spooner then turned her attention to Amos Bright.

"I have heard rumors that you yearn to travel again, Counsel Bright. Is that true?" Her question caught him off guard.

"I uh...Well, I cannot deny that at times I miss the life," Bright answered, perhaps too quickly. "But my work here is most interesting and I..." Spooner raised her translucent palm to silence him. Her silky outer robe slid back, revealing a thin pale arm adorned with the markings of a Priest of The Master's House—the highest religious order on Antares. Ruth Charnofsky took notice. Spooner held a higher status in Antarean society than she had imagined. The marking placed her at the very apex of the planet's power structure. Although this High Council, and others subservient to it in all Antarean cities, was the public face of government, they were controlled by a conclave of newly anointed and self-appointed techno-priests—a throwback to the old religious power structure. But instead of worship of The Master, they attributed all to technology that The Master provided. The impending leap to intergalactic travel was, they had proclaimed, the ultimate proof of their direct ties to The Master's work.

"We appoint Counsel Amos Bright, Ambassador to the Sloor of Klane, in the Rigel system of our Galaxy. On behalf of Antares, you will carry our official greeting to our new friends, the Sloor."

The rest of the council stood and emitted a high pitched, howling sound—the Antarean sign of great approbation.

Humbly, Amos Bright rose and bowed to Spooner. "I am honored to be chosen, Head Counsel."

"Yes. Yes. A great honor," Spooner muttered, as she set aside the papers in front of her and gazed down sternly at the five Brigade commanders standing before her. Her silence spoke volumes. These five Earth-humans, and their whole Brigade, troubled her. "And now, let us join the great gathering and pay our respects to the Geriatric Brigade for their outstanding work on behalf of all Antarean Councils," Spooner proclaimed. She then adjourned the meeting.

CHAPTER NINE
A SECRET EXPOSED

After Bernie Lewis had processed Joe Finley's entire message from Klane, he revealed its contents to Rose, but told no one else. He knew the children were aware of the commanders' new communication ability, but they did not mention it to him during lunch, and he did not broach the subject. Joe Finley's message regarding the children's involvement with the Sloor confirmed Bernie's suspicions.

A planning session to receive the visitors from Antares took most of the afternoon. The staff and children met on the western patio of Butterfly House, overlooking the cove, dock and beach. They worked until sunset. There would be more than fifty beings to bring down from the Mothership—parents, commanders, Antarean medical officers and perhaps observers from the Antarean High Council. The mission's sole purpose was to test the children. Based on the results, their future would be determined. But from the moment the meeting began, it was clear that the children were going to have a major say in that future.

"Can't the Mothership come here directly?" Beam Amato asked. "No. This is one of the new inter-galactic vessels.

They are much larger and might be detected. It will likely moon-park on the dark side," Philip Margolin told her.

"Agreed," Alicia Sanchez Margolin added. "We can shuttle everyone down here with our Probeship at night. At the time of the estimated arrival, the Persieds radiant meteor shower will be at its peak. It's a perfect cover."

"Or, if we get bad weather, they can be brought down in daytime," Philip added.

"None of that is necessary," Bernie Lewis said. "This Mothership carries Shuttlecraft and Probeships that are capable of masking. Our visitors will make their way down to us themselves."

"What about Gideon Mersky?" Eric Erhardt asked.

"What about him?" Bernie responded, wondering how the children knew Mersky was on Antares. Amos Bright had used Jack Fischer to contact the retired Defense Secretary. Perhaps they picked up the information from Phil Doyle, Jack's close friend who was currently visiting Butterfly House.

"Is he coming here?" The more intense Joshua Erhardt, Eric's twin, spoke up. His talents as a seer and sensitive were well established.

"I have not heard," Bernie answered honestly.

"And, Uncle Bernie," Eric chimed in. "Can you tell us why that Gideon Mersky may be processed to commander?" The question surprised Bernie. He no idea that anyone had offered Mersky a Brigade commander's position.

"I know nothing about that either," Bernie said. "Where did you guys hear all this?" The children remained silent. "Okay," Bernie continued, still trying to avoid confrontation. "I'll check it out and let you know."

"It might be dangerous for him to come here," Melody Messina said. Was this a threat, Bernie wondered? Where were the children's questions coming from? And why?

"Dangerous, Melody?" Rose asked. "Why would he be dangerous? And to whom?"

"He doesn't know that we are here," Melody answered.

"That's true," Bernie said, still unsure what the children were after.

"I imagine since that information was kept from him, he might be angry about it," Melody continued. "And with the powers of a commander...well, he could make trouble."

"What kind of trouble?" Phil Margolin asked with growing alarm, concerned that the children were being unusually assertive. Melody hesitated a moment, as if silently checking with her siblings in a manner the Lewises could not detect.

"We think it is possible that he might want us, at least some of us, to remain behind on Earth," she finally answered.

Rose was curious about Melody's response. Why would Mersky want that to happen? He couldn't overrule Chief Commander Ruth Charnofsky, or the Antarean Mothership Commander, whoever that might be. But before Rose could say anything, Alicia Margolin spoke up.

"And what, may I ask, is wrong with that? Earth is, after all, your home planet. With the abilities you have, it might be a very positive thing for some of you to remain behind." The children immediately reacted negatively to her suggestion. They shook their heads, uttering several idiomatic objections.

"No way...We're out of here...Forget about it..." For the first time, in a long time, they sounded like children their age. Bernie decided to use their outburst to get some control on the situation.

"Fine...fine," he told them. "This is all conjecture. It will be discussed if...if you're able to travel off-planet."

"And that's a big if," Philip Margolin chimed in.

"That decision does not lie in your hands, Uncle Phil," Beam Amato told her teacher, "or anyone else's." Her attitude was firm, but not disrespectful. It made Philip Margolin uneasy. New tension seeped into the meeting, and something more. Bernie and Rose sensed resistance emanating from the children, en masse.

"Okay. Let's all calm down," Bernie suggested, trying to defuse the situation. He was not ready for an outright confrontation. "Any talk of leaving, or staying, is premature. The fact is, we don't know if space travel is in the cards for you guys yet, now do we? We don't know what your parents, or the commanders, or the Antareans will find." There was an awkward silence. The children glanced furtively at one another. Another secret signal? They kept their thoughts to themselves. "So how about we just be patient and see what develops?"

"Fine, Uncle Bernie," Joshua Erhardt said calmly, speaking for the group. "You're right, as usual."

"Of course," Bernie said with a wry smile. "Now, I have something important to tell you," he continued, speaking slowly and carefully, opening his mind to receive signals from the children, should any care to give them. "I have a message today from Commander Joe Finley on Klane..."

"My parents are there!" Beam Amato blurted out. A few silently told her to be quiet. Bernie noted the command, but could not determine who gave it.

"Yes they are. And your namesake, Antarean commander Beam, leads them. They won't be here for this visit."

"I'll see them on Klane," Beam said matter-of-factly.

"Well, yes. I hope so," Bernie said sincerely. "Commander Finley's message is clear." He chose his next words carefully. "There has been an emergence of a species, a race on Klane called Sloor. These beings seem to be on a course of rapid evolution at a rate much faster than is normal in the general scheme of things."

"Perhaps it's an anomaly, Uncle Bernie," Scott Green interjected. He was bright and handsome—the spitting image of his father, Brigade Commander Ben Green. Although Melody Messina and the Erhardt twins spoke for the group, Bernie suspected that Scott might be the children's unannounced leader.

"Perhaps," Bernie answered, "but they have metamorphosed from batrachian to ornithological, from gill to lung breathing, from cold to warm-blooded, from primitive-communicative to telepathic—all in just two generations. That's unheard of in all Antarean space travel experience."

"What do the Antareans think is happening?" Melody asked cautiously.

"They're not sure. No one in the Brigade is either." Bernie felt he had to be very careful. Joe Finley's message was still out there as a transmission. He knew that if the children had the ability to find it, they would.

"Do they have any theories?" Melody asked.

"It is possible that their evolutionary leap has been assisted in some way the Antareans don't yet understand."

"Assisted? How?" Scott asked. Bernie continued slowly and deliberately.

"Well, Scott...It seems while in their transitory period under their ocean, the Sloor have had outside contact. Human contact. Earth-human contact."

Melody and Beam exchanged a quick glance, as did several of the others. Bernie detected a slight blush rise on the cheeks of Eric Erhardt.

"What exactly is it that you're telling us, Uncle Bernie?" Scott Green asked in a way that was clear he was speaking on behalf of the group.

"Just what the message said. It appears that some of you, perhaps all of you, have been in contact with the Sloor. I don't understand how or why. And more importantly, we don't understand why you have kept this from us!"

CHAPTER TEN
THE GATHERING

The hundreds of Brigade members gathered in the Antarean's great meeting hall were a sight to behold. The last time so many of them were together was at the end of their orientation on Antares, twenty-one Earth-years ago. Many had not seen one another since then. People who had once retired to South Florida for the condo life, or were resigned to a life's end of assisted living, or neglectful nursing home care, now robustly and heartily embraced one another and renewed old friendships.

They discussed the systems, planets, species, races, cultures and civilizations they had visited and worked among. There was very little talk about their past life on Earth, even though many had left families behind. Secret communication, done through Jack Fischer, via Bernie Lewis, allowed any who wished to keep in touch back home. Others, whose families had neglected or abandoned them in old age, never looked back on their Earthly lives, but rejoiced in their rebirth in the Universe.

Singles, widows, and widowers, many of them now coupled with humanoids from around the galaxy's planetary systems, introduced their mates. The temperature, gravity and atmospherics of the great hall were kept Earthly. For those non-Earth humanoids who required them, special breathing, pressure and gravity apparatus were provided by the Antareans.

Those couples who had left their babies behind at Butterfly House sought out each other. They excitedly discussed the impending trip to Earth, and the long awaited reunion with their children.

The hall was charged with festive excitement and energy. The amenities in the hall had been thoughtfully provided by their Antarean hosts. Among these, the food was the biggest hit. It included favorites such as deep-crust pizza, hamburgers, southern fried chicken, Philadelphia cheese-steaks and several Cantonese and Szechwan Chinese dishes—tastes from another time and place; another lifetime.

Panatoy, the Subaxian who had mated with Chief Commander Ruth Charnofsky, chatted with some Brigade members who had served on his planet years ago. His breathing device was on minimal setting because of the carbon dioxide being generated by so many Earth-humans. But the incandescent light was beginning to cause his ultraviolet sensitive skin to itch.

Panatoy ignored the problem as he waited impatiently for Ruth and the other Brigade Commanders to return from their meeting with the Antarean High Council. Then the tall chemist, taller than any adult Antarean, saw Amos Bright enter the hall escorting an Earth-human that Panatoy vaguely recognized. His interest was tweaked as he watched Bright introduce the man to several of the Brigade guests. He took note that they did not greet the stranger with the same warmth or enthusiasm that they held for one another. Their response was polite, but cold. He was obviously not a Brigade member. Although considered impolite to do so, Panatoy's acute sense of hearing enabled him to eavesdrop. He listened intently as Bright approached the group that had arrived on the Shar-Barkat transport.

"I believe you know Gideon Mersky," Amos Bright said to the group that included Annabella Costa. Several nodded. Annabella smiled.

"Why, of course we do, Counsel Bright," she said with her syrupy southern drawl. She had deliberately kept it as a reminder of her past and as a playful irritant to some of the "Yankee" Brigade members. "Why dear Mr. Mersky and I met on that utterly dreary Shar-Bakart transport."

She stepped closer to Mersky and offered her hand. "Shall we have that dance y'all promised me, Mr. Secretary?" He followed her lead, smiling sheepishly back at the others, as Annabella led him away onto the dance floor.

The Antareans had done their best to recreate an Earth-like ambiance in the great hall. A large mirrored sphere hung from the ceiling. Colorful incandescent lights were aimed at it; their reflections scattered multi-colored moving pinpoints over and above the gathering. The effect was much like a ballroom, circa 1930.

The music consisted of original radio broadcasts captured from that era by Antarean deep-space modulation scanners, a device they had developed to determine signs of life on planets. There were several civilizations in the galaxy able to capture electronic transmissions, and emissions, from distant sources. The Antareans had perfected a process of recording these and rejuvenating the original sounds and pictures to extremely high definition and quality.

The current selection was a pleasing mix of the Glenn Miller and Count Basie bands interspersed with ballads by Frank Sinatra, Tony Bennett, and Ella Fitzgerald.

Round tables, seating groups of thirty, surrounded the vast dance floor that was now packed with swaying Brigade couples. The china, silverware, tablecloths and napkins were exact copies garnered from a 1955 *Good Housekeeping Magazine* issue that featured elegant table settings. The centerpieces were Turlian duplications of Lilies of the Valley and American Beauty Roses, set off with sprigs of white Baby's Breath and pink Astilbe framed with ferns. They felt real to the touch. Their fragrances were everywhere.

Artificial sunlight and temperature were matched to that of January in Southern Florida, where most of the Brigade had originated. With the exception of two discoveries of rare, water/oxygen planets similar to Earth, most Brigade members had not been in such a familiar environment since they left home. Most had served on planets with caustic atmospheres, major geological disruptions, multiple suns and moons, increased or decreased gravitational pulls or severe weather, worked on brutally hot desert planets that were a common occurrence in a universe where liquid water was a rarity. Some planets had atmospheres and weather so hostile that on occasion even the impervious hull-seals of Antarean Motherships had nearly been compromised.

The homey setting reminded all how far they'd traveled from what were to be their "golden years" on Earth, as senior citizens. Now they were all vital and energetic deep-space ambassadors and teachers with an indeterminate life span ahead of them.

Two unfortunate mishaps had claimed twelve of their number. During an exploratory landing on planet Pelli, in the Alphard solar system, an unexpected volcanic eruption occurred directly under a shuttlecraft, moments after landing and shutdown. Four were lost there. And an older Mothership, returning from the ice-moon Callo, in Orion, was overcome by a proton storm emanating from a nearby blue dwarf star as it went nova. Eight Brigade members perished instantly. In both instances, no parents of Butterfly House children were involved.

Myriad dangers that accompany journeys through the galaxy, or work on harsh worlds were part of the Brigade's daily life. They had all adjusted to the possibility of encountering danger, and accepted the challenge. Now, the thought of exploring beyond their own galaxy increased their excitement and aroused their curiosity.

But among those lost, three couples had family members on Earth. Details of the tragedies were sent to Bernie Lewis. He then had Jack Fischer deliver the sad news to the families. Most knew of their relatives' decision to leave Earth, and had sworn to keep the secret. But nearly twenty years had now passed. The image they had was of their relatives as elderly, and frail, close to the end of their lives. Most family members took the news of the accidents in stride, knowing their relatives had gone into space voluntarily. A few still refused to believe such events had occurred and, although they treated Jack Fischer politely, they maintained that their loved ones had passed on and out of their lives long ago.

Commander Frank Hankinson's philosophical take on that attitude was, "Well, I guess we're a bit distant from South Florida, but at least we're not attending a funeral once a week anymore while that's all they have to look forward to."

Annabella Costa's curvaceous body, wrapped in a silken blue evening gown, felt familiar and pleasant to Gideon Mersky as she snuggled against him on the dance floor. The music was from Frank Sinatra's

1958 *Wee Small Hours* album. They did a fox trot to the title tune. Annabella's hair smelled of mint and lavender—a sexual stimulant to Mersky's memory of their love-making on the Shar-Bakart transport. They had not been together now for six days. He was aroused. Feeling his response, she pressed harder against him.

"I missed you too, Pumpkin," she whispered in his right ear. Her breath was warm and sweet.

"Mmmm..." was all he could muster. The reawakened sexual feelings rising in him were still wondrous. He reveled in the feeling.

"Where did y'all disappear to after we docked?" she asked.

"I had some, uh...business. With the Antareans..." Her generous breasts rubbed against him as they turned and dipped. His knee slid softly up against her groin. He lifted her, enjoying the strength of his arms. Her eyes smiled. "What?" he asked, enjoying the sensation of her nearness and her female scent.

"Listen up, Honey-Bun. We all have 'business,' as you say, with the Ants. I thought we...you and me...well, I figured y'all was fixin' to be with me. You take my meanin'?" She gently pulled away from his embrace. They stopped dancing and stood swaying in place.

"Of course I was. I am..." he said, looking back into her large, fetching, brown eyes. "But I'm his guest and..."

"Amos Bright's guest?"

"Yes."

"He's a big mucky-muck. On their High Council, you know."

"I know. So what?" She studied Mersky's face. His intelligent, piercing, hazel eyes revealed nothing. A stoic, almost blank expression hid his true nature. He blocked entrance into his mind. Perhaps later, when I have him alone, Annabella thought to herself. She returned to his arms.

"So? So fiddle-dee," she said in her best Scarlet O'Hara imitation. "You're here now, and I don't want you to leave my side for the rest of this celebration. There are just too many unattached women with hot, rejuvenated libidos floating around."

"And yours isn't?" he said playfully.

"Now y'all know better than to ask a lady a question like that, Mr. Secretary." She slid her knee up between his legs.

He pressed back against her. "Yes I do, Annabella...Oh do I ever!"

"That's better, Gideon darlin'. Much better." They continued to dance close while she silently pondered what business this newcomer might have with the politically powerful Amos Bright. She glanced over at the tall Antarean and noted that in addition to his council robes, he now wore the respected insignia of Ambassador. My, my, she thought. Now aren't we moving up the ladder quickly.

Panatoy, amused and curious, kept listening and observing. He would have, as his dear mate would say, a juicy story to tell Ruth later.

CHAPTER ELEVEN
GOOD TO GO

Apopular space-physics theory among intergalactic travelers, including the Antareans, was that travel at light speed bends time, much as gravity, a force between masses, bends space. Following these theorems, travelers at light speed could gather unto themselves the mass of the universe, and thus its substance, time and distance. But when the incredible ability of the crystalline Parmans to absorb light was discovered, and tested within the Milky Way Galaxy, a new theory was formed that eventually proved to be correct.

Known as Starlight Absorption Warp (SAW), it was first proposed by the Chig-Hackla Space Center on Makk-Hallag, the ninth planet in the Pleiades system. It became a proven fact when the starlight consuming Parmans, were able to project Antarean spacecraft beyond light speed.

Before then, Antarean Motherships traveling across the galaxy at sub-light speeds spent time getting to their destinations. In other words, time passed from the moment they left a destination to the moment they arrived. With the Parman's light gathering capability, intra-galactic travel at greater than light-speed proved that time was a universal constant. Time was the same everywhere in the galaxy and, it was theorized, in the Universe.

The Antareans, under the leadership of their renowned physicist, Lage Marinin, developed and built a new navigation system and energy drive that could be coupled with Parman starlight absorption capability—the engineered realization of SAW. Marinin restated the Chig-Hackla theory this way:

"As one attains light speed, one moves from
light present toward light past, but does
not go back in time. Rather, at light speed,
time is frozen in place. As one approaches a
destination, the light from it being absorbed
by the Parmans gets younger and younger, until
upon arrival, time and space have adjusted
the traveler to the local present, which was
the same time as when light speed was first
attained. For any given time measurement,
from eon to nanosecond, time in one place in
the Universe is simultaneously the same time
in all other places. Remaining time-current,
or "on time," is only a matter of getting to
one's destination without spending time
getting there at less than light-speed.
However, one cannot go back in time this
way. The current moment cannot be replaced
by time past."

Additionally, a radically new hull design incorporated a spacecraft
skin of Herite—a new alloy consisting of fused titanium, silicon and
helium that could withstand the incredible temperatures and stresses of
faster-than-light travel. This new inter-galactic Mothership's skin also
contained properties that, when faster-than-light speed was reached,
deflected all matter. Although most of the Universe is a vacuum, it is
not a void. Objects such as nebula, stars, planets, moons, asteroids, comets and meteors were only a tiny part of its mass. Solar winds, neutrons,
protons, electrons, quarks and the ever present, changing and becoming
"stardust" were everywhere. The deflective properties of Herite served
as its own shield against almost all space debris, from huge, rogue
asteroids, to sub-atomic quarks.

Messaging across the galaxy, telepathically, by Brigade commanders
aboard a Parman driven Mothership, further confirmed the existence
of a space-time continuum. "Destination Achieved" confirmation of

messages from all corners of the galaxy arrived simultaneously to all Brigade commanders immediately after the new Antarean Motherships exceeded light-speed. The theories of relativity dealing with the masses of space and time, and quantum-mechanics dealing with the infinitesimal sub-atomic working of the universe, were thus merged into one smooth operating mode. The SAW theory that when light-speed is surpassed, time is a constant, became fact. Stating it another way—with the mass of the Universe as one, then place, like time, is always the same. The Universe appeared to be accessible and without boundary for the Parman-driven Antarean Motherships.

The Antareans had never encountered intergalactic travelers in their galaxy. So now, as they planned to venture out to other galaxies, they strongly suspected they were the first beings in the Universe to do so. If this was true, it would give them an enormous advantage among the known space explorers and traders. That advantage, along with the Geriatric Brigade commanders' communication capabilities, would give Antarean exploration of the entire Universe a unique exclusivity, or so they thought. Leaders like Spooner felt this was proof of The Master's Grand Plan. It confirmed and strengthened their belief that they were His chosen beings, destined to implement His plan universally.

While the gathering was in full swing, Spooner received word that all testing and shakedown of the two new inter-galactic Motherships had been successfully completed. She gave the order to proceed. The era of Antarean inter-galactic travel was launched. The two vessels vectored toward their jump-off points and on to their assigned galaxies. But were they, Antareans, Parmans and the Geriatric Brigade, the first to travel inter-galactic? That question was soon to be answered in a way none of the travelers suspected.

CHAPTER TWELVE
OUTREACH

The precise movements of the children during the three years they were away from Butterfly House was not clear to the Lewises, Margolins or Martindales. True, the children had kept in contact, and reported their general activities such as, "going to school," or "working in a copper mine," or "aiding refugees from Genocide," but none of their guardians had physically observed them. The children, for their own reasons, wanted it that way while they learned about their home planet and its inhabitants. After attending colleges and universities, they traveled, immersing themselves in the various cultures, religions and social structures while becoming close friends with several special young people they met. As observers, they noted stark differences and discordance between peaceful, prosperous, tolerant nations, and those steeped in bigotry, hatred and brutality. They also clearly saw how humans were destroying their environment. Many places had become unlivable. Species were becoming extinct at a rapid rate. The ability of Earth to sustain life was threatened. This behavior disturbed the children, but they did not use their powers, as they might have, to interfere. Instead, the secretly vowed to find a way to help their species survive.

The children had begun communicating with one another while still in the womb. Their embryonic brains functioned at nearly seventy percent capacity. They were able to absorb information from outside the womb in a form and language unknown to their parents. But what was happening to them stretched far beyond the place of their birth in the secretive NASA hospital wing of Building 11, in Houston.

The startling truth was that, prior to birth, these children were a new race, capable of communicating with other beings that were gestating throughout the Universe.

In-utero, in-egg or pre-divided, communication is something that all humanoid, carbon-based fetuses can do. Once born, Earth-humans, and most living creatures, do not hold conscious memory of this capacity. But the children of Butterfly House retained memory of all their intra and inter-galactic conversations and contacts. When born, their brain usage increased to ninety percent. By the time they were fifteen, it was close to ninety-five percent. They developed and honed their communication skills, focusing them to communicate individually and as a group. In doing so, they were able to keep in touch with the thousands of life forms they had met before birth across many galaxies.

Some beings remembered communicating with the children and after their birth, emergence or division, continued to do so, while others had to be taught once they emerged into their worlds. The children were excellent teachers. This celestial conversation went on among all of these far-flung young as they grew and developed. Those who procreated rapidly, like the Sloor, passed this ability on to their young.

Over many years, the thousands of living beings communicating this way, had in turn, reached out to thousands more, until an inter-galactic network, growing geometrically, spanned out to the very edges of the Universe.

Had the Antareans, the Brigade, or any other space travelers been able to eavesdrop on this inter-galactic chatter, it would have been apparent that the children of Butterfly House were leaders at the vortex of a new linking of life and future.

And something else was happening. Many of the contacts the children made were humanoid, becoming humanoid, or possessed that potential. Evolution depended greatly on environment. But another factor surfaced as the contacts increased. Beyond the ability to communicate, many beings of a like chemical and physical base shared common genetic markings and bonds.

The children understood why, and how, this had occurred. Their own genetic makeup had been altered artificially as a result of their parents being processed for deep-space travel by the Antareans. It had caused a reversal in their parents' aging processes and an increase in their own intellectual and physical potential. But it also caused far reaching genetic changes. These alterations had been passed on to the children, causing a quantum evolutionary leap—an event that might not have occurred naturally for scores of millennia, if ever.

These contacts were producing evolutionary leaps in many beings and species. True, a few were the random results of inter-planetary mating. Others, like their parents, occurred from the deep-space processing that manipulated genetic codes. But these were rare. Most rapid evolution occurred within the forces of nature when the enlightenment of the children interacted with those life forms whose one overriding purpose was to procreate and protect the species.

A few months before their tenth birthday, five children, Melissa Messina, Beam Amato, Scott Green, and the Erhardt twins, Joshua and Eric, made a startling discovery. They were able to visit other planets with their presence by a process they called projecting. As a group, with total concentration, they could leap across space, not only with their thoughts, but with a molecular essence of themselves. They could, without leaving Cayman Brac, and the safety of Butterfly House, experience a sense of place in real-time.

They practiced projecting for several weeks before teaching it to their peers. Many projections were made, including, as the Amatos and Finleys discovered, visits to the Sloor on Klane.

The children reached beyond their galaxy to many others including what Scott Green called, "The ultimate out-of-body experience." They continued experimenting; projecting further and further to what they felt might be the very edges of the Universe. But so far, although they suspected a limit, they had found no actual border, boundary or end. The Universe seemed to have no beginning, no end, and no limit—only infinity beyond infinity.

Like the children of Butterfly House, many beings and species had grown in intellectual power. Most of these were not space travelers. However, that mode of travel begged the question. Were spaceships really necessary? Contact and communicating with others by projection caused all other modes to be obsolete. But its purpose, should there be one other than a new way to evolve, was not clear to the participants.

Among the life forms, cultures and civilizations were various explanations of existence as part of a universal plan. Many had one or more religions that explained the existence of life and purpose. For those who clung tenaciously to these beliefs, an afterlife had to exist. They found the idea that conscious life ended impossible to accept. But inter-galactic communication made the concept of possessing a unique or "true" religion also difficult to accept. Once the young of so many planets, systems and galaxies became aware of one another, and of their Universe teeming with life, parochial religious concepts seemed terribly irrelevant. Most agreed that they were essentially part of a common material—stardust. That single fact embodied all reasons why life, and life's sustenance, evolved and flourished. Whether it was a Universal Grand Plan, or an accident of nature, it made no difference. Cognitive life was everywhere. Survival and procreation, driven by a genetic engine, was the common purpose. Respect for all other life was simply respect for one's own.

After mastering projection, and making so many inter-galactic friends, the children were drawn to physically leaving Earth. They had to venture into the Universe and touch it. Molecular visits were all well and good, but they craved contact—face to face, tentacle, antennae, skin, scale, bone, crystal, gaseous...they had to see. As Joshua Erhardt said, "There's just one hell of a lot of life out there to meet, greet and touch in person."

Together, with beings from across the Universe, the children of Butterfly House established a credo that they all promised to nourish and disperse to all in their common home. It was passed from being to being; from planet to planet; system to system; galaxy to galaxy and continuously projected beyond to the vast, never-ending universe:

"From Stardust we came.
And to Stardust we shall return.
The cycle is forever.
The Universe is our home, our source.

Eternal and infinite.
So it is with everyone; every being; everything.
On the journey of life, we are many, and we are one.
We are all part of one another, and everything.
Bonded and inseparable, we are, and we live—always."

CHAPTER THIRTEEN
BEZZOLENTINE AND MANIGRA

The Antareans used quadrants to chart stars, solar systems, planets, and major moon positions in their own galaxy. These were three-dimensional divisions, emanating from the geographic center point of the galaxy. They then used the quads for navigation and mapping. This program was applied to the galaxies they now entered. First, the program visualized a galaxy as a three dimensional shape, such as a ball, or disk, or hexagon. Then it sliced through the shape horizontally, creating several layers, like pies placed one on top of another. Each pie was divided in quarters, or quads. The size of the galaxy, and the number and concentration of stars and systems would then determine how many pies were required. The number of quads was four times the pie slices. So if a galaxy had ten pie slices, there would be forty quads.

Once a galactic center was determined, on-board telescopic devices and computers quickly rough-mapped the galaxy. Then, as the Mothership moved through it, sensors would constantly refine the quad maps. Thus, the more time spent in a particular quad, the more accurate the navigation and mapping. As a result, there was more capability to locate and visit promising stars, planetary systems, moons and asteroids for exploration. Additionally, the more data they gathered, the more accurate were defenses against collisions with comets, meteors, solar prominences, space storms and radiation discharges.

As the Parman Guide narrowed its ultra violet focus on a giant red star in Quad-nine, and its rate of absorption, the effect on the sleek new Antarean Mothership was a reduction from supra-light to sub-light speed. This galaxy, like all others except theirs, had no officially registered name. It was uncharted and initially identified only by number. Since it was the first, it was designated Galaxy One. More than one million light years away, the second of the new breed of Antarean Motherships was about to enter another uncharted galaxy, Galaxy Two.

The Antarean commander of this Mothership was Duartone. He was very experienced, having captained on four intra-galactic Motherships before receiving command of this new breed of spacecraft. Beside the two Parman Guides on board, there was a crew of nine Antareans and fifteen Brigade members, led by Commander Frank Hankinson. Frank's wife, Andrea, accompanied him. She was not a Brigade Commander. They had no children at Butterfly House.

Before Brigade life, Frank Hankinson was retired. He had owned an independent television station in St. Louis, Missouri; he was a self-made man who had worked his way up from cub reporter to entrepreneur. When he retired, he sold the station and sought out the fabled "good life" in South Florida. Golf, swimming, sun...fun. It didn't take long until he and Andrea were bored. Then, as so often happens, he fell ill. Retirement had nearly been a death sentence.

So when his old friend Ben Green invited the Hankinson's to join the Geriatric Brigade, it took Frank and Andrea about ten seconds of reflection before they said "Yes!" Frank's decision to become a commander took five seconds more. Frank and Andrea never regretted leaving Earth.

With the galactic center located, quad-mapping began. But first, Duartone officially named the galaxy Bezzolentine, in honor of an ancient Antarean priestly order that had codified The Master's Grand Plan. He then activated a search instrument program the Antareans called "Finder."

Before the Brigade's entry into space travel, all Antarean Finders were programmed to locate systems and planets that, within them, had an Antarean-friendly atmosphere, gravity and climate. But with Earth-humans on board, the Finder's parameters had been changed to include planets with atmospheres of high oxygen content, water, and moderate temperature.

The Finder focused on Bezzolentine, Quad-nine, and adjusted the ship's course. The mapping program began to identify, then temporarily name and number systems, planets and satellite bodies within Quad-nine. Duartone took note that the Finder chose a vector toward a cluster of stars at the edge the Quad. It showed three systems that had planets potentially within Earth-human survival parameters. Another message to change course was delivered to the Parman Guide located outside the Mothership, along with the location of the starlight to be absorbed. A moment later, the Mothership's speed increased and the huge craft was vectored toward the target.

The next instruction from Finder was to tell the Parman Guide to concentrate on a single planetary system that revolved around a Red Giant. Duartone gave one of the Brigade members working on linkage duty with the Parman Guide, the honor of naming the giant red star and system. This man, Michael O'Connell, was originally from Boston. He had been a Boston Celtics basketball fanatic. The first "red" that came into his mind was Red Auerbach, the legendary basketball coach of the Celtics. The Finder entered the name—Bezzolentine-Auerbach-Quad-nine. Moments later, as more data was gathered and refined, another command came from the Finder to the Parman Guide outside the Mothership. The seventh planet out from the planetary system fit the Earth-human parameters and was selected for exploration. Duartone gave Commander Fred Hankinson the honor of naming the planet. Keeping in tune with the sports motif set by O'Connell, and being from St. Louis and a Cardinal baseball fan, Frank named the planet for the Hall of Fame baseball player, Stan Musial.

A short time later, as the Mothership closed in on the planet, the Parman Guide was disengaged from propulsion. The ship slowed and the ion-drives took over for the final approach to Bezzolentine-Auerbach-Musial-Prima-Quad-nine. Prima, in the new name, signified this planet as the first to be explored in the Auerbach system of the newly named Bezzolentine Galaxy.

Of course, a name change was possible, once determination was made about any inhabitants and/or special physical properties of the planet. If there was life, and that life had a name for their planet, system, red giant star and galaxy, those names would be respected and replace those now registered with Finder. This would hold true for all Quads in a galaxy.

As they drew closer to planetary orbit, Duartone asked Frank Hankinson to message Antares confirming their safe arrival in Galaxy One. All identification, including naming it Bezzolentine, and the Finder's choice of a planet to explore, was to be sent. But before Brigade Commander Hankinson could proceed, the ship's universal communications console, programmed to automatically activate upon any planetary approach, received a contact from the targeted planet. Someone was welcoming Frank Hankinson by name. Then, in perfect English, the voice asked that only Brigade members descend to the planet's surface.

Over one-million-plus light years across the Universe from the Bezzolentine Galaxy, but in the same moment of time, Brigade Commander Betty Franklin was aboard the other new-generation Antarean Mothership assigned to inter-galactic exploration. This ship was captained by Antarean commander Shai-Noa, a veteran of hundreds of explorations in their own galaxy; know to Earth-humans as the Milky Way. Shai-Noa had been chosen by the High Council because of her vast experience with newly contacted beings and cultures.

Once her Mothership's Finder had roughly charted the galaxy, temporarily named Galaxy Two, Shai-Noa renamed it Manigra, in honor of the twenty-six Antareans and eight Brigade members who died three Earth-years ago when a blue dwarf star went nova. That Mothership's Antarean Commander was named Manigra-Cha.

Finder identified Quad-24 as containing potential Earth-like solar systems. On command, the Parman Guide turned the great ship toward a specific star and planetary system in Quad-24 and engaged. Upon approaching the star and system, the ion drive took over.

Brigade Commander Betty Franklin named the star Sparkle Plenty, in honor of an old Dick Tracy cartoon character from her youth. Finder then zeroed in on a likely planet. Shai-Noa named the planet Marinin, in honor of the Antarean designer, Lage Marinin, whose new Mothership navigation system and enhanced ion-energy drive now guided them toward the planet.

As the Mothership approached orbit around the oxygen/water planet, Betty Franklin, like Frank Hankinson now at Bezzolentine-Auerbach-Musial-Prima-Quad-nine, was addressed by name, in English, with a message of welcome. The voice was female and referred to the planet as Paccum. Betty connected it with pax, the Latin word for peace, and that eased her anxiety. The designation, Marinin, was dropped from the Finder's data base and replaced with Paccum. The voice then made the same request that Frank Hankinson had received one million light years away—only Brigade members could come down to the surface of Manigra-Sparkle Plenty-Paccum-Prima-Quad-twenty four at this time.

CHAPTER FOURTEEN
AN ANCIENT CODE BROKEN

Joe Finley stepped out of the shower and slipped into a white, terrycloth robe. He dried his feet and walked into the sleeping quarters he shared with his wife, Alma, who was resting on their bed.

"That felt good," he said. Alma smiled at Joe, and stretched. Her own lavender silk robe slipped open, revealing her svelte body. Joe smiled.

"What?" she asked coyly, knowing full well why he was smiling. She enjoyed the moment.

"I will be forever stunned seeing my love, now a woman of eighty, possessing a body like that." Alma, who during her life on Earth had been a TV news-anchor on a local Boston station, chuckled and shyly closed her robe. She got up and slid off the bed.

"Why thank you, Sweetheart," she said. She let her robe slip open again as she walked over to her husband, embraced him, and then kissed him softly on the mouth. "You ain't so bad looking yourself, Joe Finley," she whispered. She touched him, feeling the strength of his muscular arm through his robe. "You're what the kids used to call a hunk." Joe blushed. His wife had always been the more sexually aggressive during their years of marriage on Earth. "Now for the important question," she continued, taking her hand away from his arm. "Did you leave me any hot water? I've got the smell of that oily, ammonia-laced Klanian Sea on me."

"All you want," he answered. As she walked away toward the bathroom, he lovingly patted her rear.

"Hold that thought," she said, over her shoulder. "I don't believe we've ever made love in daytime in this system."

"Nothing like another first," he responded.

In the Antarean quarters of the Klane base, Commander Beam pondered the day's events. After the Sloor had departed on their mating flights, the juveniles remained behind. They had kept their distance from the landing party for nearly an hour. Then one of the larger females began to communicate with Marie Amato, who was recording the activities with the Antarean equivalent of a digital camera. Beam had developed a strong attachment to Marie and Paul Amato since they had honored her by naming their daughter, now at Butterfly House, after her.

"I am not mating, Mrs. Amato," the high pitched, gentle voice told Marie. "May I approach you?"

"Yes. Of course. It is welcomed," Marie answered politely, in the manner the Antareans had taught her years ago. Their approach to contact with newly discovered living beings was always polite and non-threatening. The Brigade was also taught to give the appearance of subservience, by bowing their heads and avoiding eye contact, should the being have visible ocular organs.

"I bring greetings from Beam," the young Sloor announced.

"Oh," Marie said. "Do you mean you want to communicate with our Antarean commander who is named Beam?" Marie then deferred to Beam, who was nearby. "This young Sloor wishes to talk to you, Commander Beam." Beam opened her mind to the Sloor, but heard nothing. When she tried to communicate, she met a wall of resistance. The Sloor was blocking.

"No," the young Sloor told Marie. "It is your daughter Beam that sends her greetings to you." Marie was at first confused. "This is to you, and to your husband, Paul," the young Sloor assured her. "Your daughter tells that she is well and awaits the Mothership visit." Marie Amato was stunned. She called out to Paul, who was back at the lab, and told him what she had just heard—not only about their daughter, but that a Mothership was going to Earth!

Later, when they had returned to base, Commander Beam questioned Marie Amato as to what had transpired. The Finleys had not told Beam of the children's contact with the Sloor. Marie had not been instructed to keep that a secret. She told Beam about the greeting the Sloor had from her daughter. The Antarean commander was very disturbed. If, what Marie Amato said was true, it meant that the children at Butterfly House had developed capabilities far greater than any Antarean knew. And, she reasoned, if the children had been in contact with the Sloor, perhaps they had contacted other beings and species. If so, how many? Where? And why? Had they developed the same communication abilities their parents possessed? Was it possible that they might reach out beyond their own galaxy? And why hadn't the Brigade shared this information until now?

Most disturbing of all, it meant they had broken the ancient code of greeting that the Antareans practiced, and had carefully taught the Brigade. True, the children were not officially Brigade members, but she was certain that Bernie and Rose Lewis had been instructed to teach the children the Antarean ways and codes. This code was why Counsel Amos Bright was coming to Klane—to officially greet the Sloor and welcome them into the Antarean circle of allies, friends and trading partners.

Alma Finley emerged from her shower, eagerly anticipating making love with Joe. She dried herself, and applied a touch of White Shoulders perfume. It was her last bottle from Earth. She only used it for special occasions. One day soon, she planned to wear it when they conceived a child. The Mothership going to Earth was surely a sign that the children were ready to leave. That meant it would be safe to conceive a child and have it raised on Earth for only sixteen years, maybe less, before it could join them in space.

Alma turned off the light in the bathroom and slipped off her robe. She ran her hands down her rib cage and over her hips. Yes, she did have the body of a woman forty or fifty years younger. "Sooo delightful," she mused aloud. She opened the bathroom door, expecting to find Joe in bed, feigning sleep to tease her, but eagerly awaiting her presence. Instead, she found him fully dressed, lacing up his boots.

"Now that's romantic," she grumbled. He looked up and blinked, like a deer caught in the headlights.

"Jesus! You're gorgeous!" he said, and meant it.

"Are we going on a hike first?" she asked sarcastically.

"Huh? A hike? Oh no, Sweetheart. I'm sorry. While you were in the shower, Paul Amato came by. We have to do some damage control. You'd better get dressed, pronto."

While Alma dressed, Joe explained what had transpired between the young Sloor and Marie, and how Marie had told Beam about the children's contact with the Sloor.

"Darn it, Joe! I told you we should have informed everyone to keep things close to the vest," Alma scolded.

"You were right," Joe agreed. "My goof. Let's find Beam, and see if we can smooth things over."

Joe and Alma apologized, but Beam was not willing to let it go. "I am shocked that you didn't come to me with this news. Without sharing openly, there is no trust. This is an Antarean mission. You are under my command. We must work together." Rather than a chastisement of the Finleys, it sounded as though Beam was trying to assure herself that she was in control of the situation.

"Of course, Commander Beam," Alma said. "We are so very sorry."

"Yes," Joe added quickly, "we were going to..."

"But the code is clear!" Beam interrupted, now more agitated. It was obvious the apology had no effect. "All official welcome into the Antarean circle of trade and friendship must be made by a member of the High Council or a designated ambassador."

"We know that," Joe said. "It was as great a surprise to us as..." Beam interrupted again.

"Was it? Was it really?" Alma tried again to assuage her anger.

"Commander Beam, we had no idea the children could communicate this way... Or this far." Beam ignored her plea.

"They broke the code of greeting. That is a serious offense."

"That seems to be true," Joe responded. "But we didn't know...The Sloor inferred that the children greeted them into a much larger family. A family beyond Antares."

"Beyond?" Beam was concerned. More questions to be answered. Beyond? Had the children of Butterfly House contacted and allied with other space travelers? From where? And how far did their contact go? Could they, like the Brigade commanders, communicate across galaxies? "Who else knows about this?" she asked.

"No one off-planet," Joe lied. Alma understood why. They had to consult the other Brigade commanders, especially the Lewises, before this went any further.

"I want you to message these events to Antares," Beam ordered. "I want Counsel Bright, Ambassador to Klane, to have this news before he departs for this planet." She was certain the High Council would have new orders for him and for all intra-galactic missions; perhaps even the inter-galactic ones now underway. "Who knows?" she continued in an accusatory manner, "Who knows what other damage these children might have done, or what mischief they are up to?"

As Joe and Alma Finley formed a response to Beam's accusations they were all interrupted by a communication from Paul and Marie Amato, on duty at the site of the Sloor emergence.

"The Sloor are returning from their mating flight!" There was palpable excitement in Marie Amato's voice. "Oh, my dear God! The sky is filled with them. There are thousands. Thousands. And they are singing! Joyfully! Can you hear them?"

CHAPTER FIFTEEN
ARRIVAL ON LIAST

A few moments before dawn, the landing party of five Brigade members, led by Commander Frank Hankinson, exited their shuttlecraft and set foot on Bezzolentine-Auerbach-Musial-Prima-Quad-nine. The Finder had chosen a reasonably flat basin surrounded by rolling hills and sparse vegetation. In the distance, were forested mountains. The atmosphere was oxygen rich and breathable; the climate temperate. Humidity readings confirmed an abundance of water on the planet. Gravity was comfortable.

As they gathered in a circle around their leader, dawn broke. Because of the size of the planet's red giant star, it was a dawn that went from blue-black, to pink, to bright red, in less two minutes—their first sunrise in a new galaxy. Frank spoke with emotion and ceremony.

"We are travelers from the Milky Way Galaxy, representing the Antarean High Council and our Brigade. It is with humility and a sense of great privilege that I announce our arrival on this, the first planet reached from our galaxy to this one. We come in peace and offer friendship."

The landing party patiently awaited contact from the inhabitants who had greeted them aboard the Mothership when they first entered a planetary orbit. Frank sent out the Antarean universal greeting every five minutes, but there was no response. The red sun rose higher in the sky. There were sightings of bird-like creatures and some evidence of small land animals scurrying about.

Above, the Mothership completed her nineteenth orbit of the planet and a detailed topographical mapping of the surface. There were indications of several cities and towns. Mission Commander Duartone studied the information and then passed it down to Frank Hankinson.

The data regarding the planet's flora and fauna was transmitted to Andrea Hankinson, who was the mission's biologist.

"This is a rich planet," she told her husband as he pondered a route to the nearest settlement. Frank was growing impatient, anxious to meet the being who had greeted him. "More than two thousand various life-forms have already been identified and catalogued," Andrea continued. Frank wasn't too surprised. The atmosphere, soil, water, and sunlight, albeit in the red spectrum, held all the necessities for abundant life. It was a familiar occurrence in his own galaxy.

As Frank was briefing four Brigade members for a scouting party, a land vehicle appeared on the crest of a hill to the east. As before, a voice greeted them in English.

"Welcome to Liast, Geriatric Brigade Commander Frank Hankinson. Welcome on behalf of our government and leaders. May we approach?" The sight and sound of beings in another galaxy sent a shiver down Frank's spine. Adrenaline coursed through his body. This was the first time a Brigade commander was allowed to greet a new species on behalf of the Antareans.

"Yes. Please approach." The vehicle, a diminutive metallic hover transport, glided down the hill toward them. As it did, Frank forwarded the planet's name that the inhabitant used, Liast, up to the Mothership's Finder. Bezzolentine-Auerbach-Musial-Prima-Quad-nine immediately became Bezzolentine/Auerbach/Liast/Prima-Quad-nine. The information was logged in and coded Bezo/Auer/Liast-Pr-Q-9.

The vehicle came to a stop and settled to the ground. Its engine shut down. A door in the front opened and two Liastans emerged. Compared to Earth-humans, they were very small; about three feet. Their two eyes were wide apart and large, wrapping around their nearly perfectly round heads, giving them the ability to see forward three dimensionally, as well as individually on either side, like birds. Their mouths were small and close to the bottom of their faces. They had no chins. Frank could not see any nostrils until one Liastan turned around. They were in the rear of their heads, and quite large, with flaps that opened and closed with each deep breath, much like a whale's blow-hole. One of the Liastans stepped forward and spread his short, stubby arms. He then extended his surprisingly large, seven-fingered hands outward, palms up, in the universal sign of greeting and peace.

"Welcome to Liast, Commander Frank Hankinson. We welcome you and send you greetings from the children of Butterfly House." Hank was stunned. Duartone, who was monitoring the conversation aboard the Mothership, knew nothing of the children. He thought the Liastan was referring to the young people on Liast.

"We thank you," Hankinson answered while returning the universal peace sign to the Liastan. "Now I understand how it is you know my native language."

"Yes. Your children taught us. We are anxious to meet them in person. Do you know when they are coming?"

"What is this one talking about?" Duartone telepathed down to Frank. "What children?"

"It's a long story. If the High Council approves, I'll fill you in later," was his silent answer. As he sent it, he wondered if the Liastans were telepathic beings. Frank studied their features for a sign that they had heard his telepath to Duartone, but there was nothing apparent to suggest they had.

Duartone, who had been so disturbed that the Liastans invited only Brigade people down to the surface, was now doubly annoyed that Commander Hankinson and the Antarean High Council had withheld important information from him. Who were these children and what was Butterfly House? But he accepted that this was not the time, nor place, to press for explanations. The primary mission was to make friends with this newly discovered race on behalf of the Antarean civilization and its interests. Yet, as this was an initial inter-galactic mission, he did not want to set precedent either. The dilemma was solved graciously by Frank Hankinson.

"I am not the leader of this mission," Frank explained to the Liastan. "So, on behalf of the Antarean High Council, and my leader, Mission Commander Duartone the Antarean, I greet you and offer you the friendship and the inter-galactic facilities of the Antarean race." Both Liastans stepped forward and bowed.

"I am Tellic," the one who had been speaking responded.

"And I am Shinner," said the second, "the leader of our city. We welcome you. It would please us if you would come with us now."

"That will be out pleasure," Shinner. Tellic then touched a device on his clothing. A much larger hover craft appeared on top of the hill and descended toward the group.

"This vehicle will accommodate your landing party," Tellic said. "The journey is short." The larger craft settled to the ground and its door opened.

"Please enter," Shinner said. As the Brigade members walked toward the vehicle, Shinner walked with Frank.

"There are others from our galaxy, and three other galaxies, in residence with us at this time. They knew of your journey and are here to greet you. Like many beings in our Universe who have been contacted by your offspring in Butterfly House, they have many questions to ask regarding your children."

CHAPTER SIXTEEN
THE GATHERING CONCLUDES

The Brigade's reunion gala was winding down by the time Head Counsel Spooner and the rest of the Antarean High Council made their entrance. They were met with applause and cheers for the up-coming trip to Earth. Panatoy was still observing Amos Bright's activities. Ruth had asked him to keep an eye on Spooner as well. He enjoyed the role and was happy to oblige. Being a chemist wasn't nearly as much fun as using his ultra-sensitive sight and hearing to gather information for his dear mate and her Brigade. So, with his tall, thin, blue body, now covered with a suit that protected his sensitive skin from the hall's incandescent light, and towering above everyone in the hall, Panatoy feigned boredom and tuned in on the activities of Amos Bright, Spooner, and if they were close, other members of the Antarean High Council.

Spooner graciously greeted as many Brigade members as she could. Her thin lips spread across her narrow face in a frozen, perpetual smile. Her narrow, tapered fingers barely touched Earth-human flesh as she glided through the hall.

Amos Bright, who had been seated with Ben and Mary Green and three of the parents of children at Butterfly House, noted Spooner's arrival and excused himself to join her and the other council members. As he did, Bright scanned the hall. His senses delineated between the body temperature of Earth-humans and the cooler Antareans. His height, well over seven feet, allowed him a good view of the crowd. Many had returned to dancing and eating. He looked to see if any Brigade commanders were watching him, but all were involved in conversation. He ignored Panatoy, whose height was a bit more than Bright's. He took notice that the Subax chemist stood next to Ruth and seemed bored.

It took a moment for Bright to locate Gideon Mersky, who was still in the clutches of Annabella Costa. He caught Mersky's eye and beckoned him. Bright was suspicious of Costa's sexual control over Mersky. He made a mental note to look into her Brigade record.

"Duty calls," Mersky told his paramour. "I have to see Amos Bright for a moment." Annabella smiled, as she glanced at the tall Antarean Counsel.

"I did notice that, Darlin'. Your master calls." Her voice was soft, but Mersky didn't miss the cynical edge of her words. He moved away from her quickly.

Panatoy bent over and whispered to Ruth that Bright and Mersky were on the move. She watched the two meet and exchange a brief word, then walk together toward the advancing Spooner.

"Listen to them carefully, Panatoy, my love. It is most important." The Subaxian nodded and raised himself to his full height.

"I have the great pleasure of introducing Gideon Mersky, Head Counsel Spooner," Bright said, as he bowed respectfully. "Mister Mersky is our first non-Brigade Earth-human visitor." Spooner extended her hand.

"Welcome to Antares, Mister Mersky. Counsel Bright has told me you will be joining the Brigade."

"Thank you, Ma'am. It is a fascinating pleasure to be here. I had no idea..."

"No," Spooner interrupted, "how could you?" For a moment, Mersky was taken aback. Had the Head Counsel been rude to him, or was her curt remark an Antarean joke of sorts?

"You're right, Ma'am. I could not. Not in my wildest dreams imagine..."

"I understand you will become a Brigade commander."

"Mr. Bright has made that suggestion. I am willing to do whatever I can to help you and your people...especially with inter-galactic communication and exploration. I am at your service." Spooner turned to Bright.

"Counsel Bright. In view of recent developments, I suggest you proceed with processing Mister Mersky to Brigade commander as quickly as possible."

Bright was about to inform Spooner of the Brigade commanders resistance to having Mersky join the Brigade, much less as a commander, but thought better of it. This was not the time, nor place, for that discussion. Brigade people might be listening. Spooner took her leave, offering Mersky her hand once more. She then moved to the front of the hall, to address the gathering. A reverberating gong sounded, drawing the gathering's attention to Spooner. The hall grew silent. Spooner raised her hands in the universal sign of greeting.

"Members of the Antarean, Earth-human, Geriatric Brigade. On behalf of the High Council, I wish to offer my congratulations on a successful reunion, and our deepest gratitude to you for all that you have meant to our universal mission." The hall erupted in applause. "You have the honor to be present on Antares this very special day. At this moment, for the first time, our civilization is reaching beyond our galaxy to others. This great leap, made possible by the generosity of our friends the Parmans, our superior space travel technology, and the inter-galactic communication skills of your commanders, is only a beginning. The entire universe now lies open before us. Let us continue, as we have for the past sixteen Earth-years, to travel together as partners, into the future The Master has ordained." There was more applause, with a few whistles and shouts. "You are a very special race that The Master has delivered into our safekeeping. May The Master always protect all of you, and your progeny, through the ages." Spooner bowed and spread her hands again in a universal sign of peace.

The Brigade members responded with several minutes of genuine applause and cheers. Ruth Charnofsky, and the other commanders present, put their hands together politely. They silently signaled to one another to meet in Ruth's quarters after the party.

When Spooner, Bright, and the other Antarean High Council members left the hall, the partying resumed for a few more hours. Some of the Brigade could not get enough of the Earthly food. Others, the more loquacious, talked endlessly of the fascinating adventures they had enjoyed throughout the galaxy. And those parents who would soon make the journey to Earth, enthusiastically made plans and traded stories about contacts with their children over the years. But none of them, as instructed, mentioned the children of Butterfly House to Gideon Mersky. His ignorance of Butterfly House also meant that Amos Bright and the Antareans had also kept the secret.

As a professional politician, Mersky understood the importance of building a base of support. Amos Bright had suggested that he might encounter opposition to his joining the Brigade as a commander. Mersky's plan was to mingle and renew old acquaintances with those he had met before—the parents who had their babies on Earth sixteen years ago. He also wanted to make friends with many other Brigade members he had never met. Bright had encouraged him to do this, secretly hoping that someone in the Brigade might inadvertently reveal that the children were still on Earth, and thus relieve him of having to break the vow of secrecy he had taken by telling Mersky himself.

But Annabella Costa had other plans for Gideon Mersky. She had received orders from Ruth Charnofsky.

"Besides keeping an eye on Gideon's movements," Ruth had told Annabella, "we would like you to see what you can learn about his plans, should he become a commander." Annabella was a crafty woman. Her years of working as a stripper had hardened her to the advances of men, and schooled her in how to use her feminine wiles to control them.

"Listen, Ruth Darlin'," she had replied to Chief Commander, who had been a very staid and proper woman on Earth, "Y'all have come to the right person for that mission. For sure, for sure."

She smiled and bent close to Ruth's ear. "If there's one thing I can get from a man, besides attention and gettin' his blood up, is a loose tongue and his confidence."

"Then your being on that Shar-Bakart transport that picked him up was provident," Ruth told her.

"Yes, Ma'am," a smiling Annabella Costa had answered.

"Just part of the good ol' Masser's plan, as our Ant buddies might say."

121

Annabella quietly slipped up behind Mersky a moment after Bright had left.

"I think it's time that you and I sashayed out of here, Lover Boy," Annabella whispered into his ear.

"Just a little while longer, Love," he answered, gently slipping his arm around her waist and pulling her close against him. "I want to talk to some of these folks about..." Annabella pulled away. Her eyes narrowed.

"Y'all decide, here and now. If'n you want to do talky-talk, I'm gonna pick myself up and do a walky-walk. And that might be a real long one, if you take my meanin'."

Mersky saw she was serious. His libido overpowered reason. They quickly left, arm in arm. Ben Green, who had observed the exchange, smiled to himself, remembering the fascination he had with his own sexual rejuvenation. He was aware of Ruth's orders to Annabella and admired the way she relentlessly kept her hooks in Mersky.

Ruth also noted the departure of the lovers and sent Annabella a secret message of approval and thanks. None of the Brigade commanders has lost their distrust of the retired Secretary of Defense. None had forgotten his attempt to forcefully keep the children on Earth, and even though he supposedly saw the errors of his ways, and apologized, they were still wary.

After the reunion gala ended, the five Brigade commanders met in Ruth's and Panatoy's suite. The Subaxian scanned the rooms for listening devices. It was clean. The Antareans, for all their intense concentration on successful exploration and trade, were, for the most part, ethical beings. They all settled into two plush sofas, facing each other. Coffee, tea and cookies were available on a silver platter that took up most of the small table between them.

"I am convinced that Spooner and the High Council have grown mistrustful of us," Ruth began

"And the children too, I gather," Art Perlman added as he stirred his coffee.

"You can't really blame the Ants," Ben Green said. "These folks have been tooling around this galaxy for millennia. They have a strong, proprietary interest in keeping the status quo."

"Yes, Ben. But apparently the kids have been doing some tooling around too," Bess said with a grin.

"I'd say more than some," Mary Green added.

"That's for sure," Ruth said. "But let's talk about the reaction of Spooner and the High Council first."

"Like I said, they're used to being in control," Ben responded. "Then, sort of overnight, Parman Guide propulsion and our communication, uh, abilities shall we say, opens up the Universe to them. And remember, not only are we their only communication link between galaxies, but they are aware we have developed a close relationship with the Parmans. I'd be nervous too."

"I think Bess and my volunteering to handle communications from Klane, calmed their fears, don't you, Ruth?" Art asked.

"Absolutely. And I think it critical that we continually assure them that we are on their side and eager to help."

"How did that become such a pressing concern?" Mary asked.

"When it became known that the children have been communicating with beings throughout the galaxy," Ruth answered. She then reiterated the total message received from Joe Finley to Bernie. "I had no choice but to make Spooner aware before Amos Bright left as Ambassador for Klane."

"Why?" Art asked.

"Because Commander Beam learned about the children's contact with the Sloor from Marie Amato. It was a mistake. No one warned Marie. Beam sent that information via the Antarean's galactic communication system. If she found out that way, she would have known we were keeping important information from her and who knows what that might have precipitated. Remember, we have commanders on the inter-galactic missions. Anyway, I spoke to her a short while ago in her quarters."

"Ruth did the right thing. She's correct about the children," Bess Perlman said. "Mary and I were talking about that at the dinner. Tell everyone what you thought, Mary." Mary Green shifted uneasily on the downy pillow. She glanced at her husband, nervously. She felt a little insecure. It was a throwback to the days when Ben was a major advertising executive and she was the stay-at-home housewife/mother who couldn't handle her empty nest when their daughters had grown up and left. She had taken to drinking alcohol and ruminating about their son, Scott, who had been killed in the Vietnam War. Now, with the prospect of being reunited with their new son, Scott, named for the one they lost, Mary didn't want anything to interfere with their trip home to Earth.

"I was telling Bess that in the Council meeting I sensed the Antareans suspect we commanders knew something about the children and that we were keeping it from them in order to circumvent their authority. They couldn't have possibly known about the Sloor because we got Joe's message just before the meeting. Of course, that was before Ruth told Spooner about the Sloor and the children..."

"Yes," Ruth admitted. "The news from Frank and Betty when they reach their respective galaxies will be ours exclusively... for the moment." Ruth got up and stood beside Panatoy. He took her hand in his. "The contacts the children seem to have made," she continued, "and the way they are refusing to be tested, as well as their insistence that we all come immediately, worries Spooner." Mary Green sipped her coffee and threw a quick glance at Ben. He was listening to Ruth respectfully. She was nervous that Ruth might postpone the trip to Earth. "Even Amos Bright, whom I regard as a friend, has a different attitude toward us. He is distant and suspicious," Ruth said.

"Not to mention he's become a champion of having Gideon Mersky join the Brigade as a commander," Panatoy chimed in. The tall blue Subax, whose long, white, silky hair flowed down and below his broad shoulders, had been standing quietly, holding his wife's hand. Although the Antareans had constructed an adjacent suite to accommodate Panatoy with comfortable Subaxian environment, he chose to wear a protective garment and portable breathing device and join the meeting. "I watched them, Bright and Mersky, with Spooner. They want him to be processed as commander immediately."

"Spooner said that?" Ben Green asked.

"Absolutely." Panatoy smiled proudly. "They were most secretive about it, but in the thick, Earth-like atmosphere of the hall I heard all their words."

"They are pushing him through to intercept our communications," Art said. "You are right, Ruth. They don't trust us."

"We cannot allow Mersky to be processed," Ruth stated categorically.

"How can we stop them?" Art asked. Panatoy spread his arms out to their full eleven-foot span.

"If I may say, I do not think it wise to confront Spooner now. You do not have enough information about her plans."

"I agree," Ben said. "We must first understand what the children have been up to and why."

"They are being strangely tight-lipped," Ruth said. "Even our daughter, Autumn, who speaks with the children regularly, would not share any information with us."

"Look," Ben then said. "The kids have found a way to reach out to the Sloor. If they can do that, then they have done it in other systems... maybe even other galaxies. So, it seems to me, that ability makes our messaging sort of obsolete, doesn't it?" They nodded their agreement. "Then giving Mersky a commander's abilities becomes moot."

"Yes," Ruth agreed. "It's the children Spooner wants to control now."

"Then the mission to Earth must go forward as quickly as possible," Bess said. "We can't allow anything to get in its way." An uneasy silence fell over the group.

"Amos Bright is Gideon Mersky's sponsor," Panatoy finally said. "And Spooner is with him on making Mersky a commander. That is very clear. But why is Bright pushing so hard? We are his friends. He is responsible for our being here, and for you, the commanders, possessing the powers you do."

"Is he doing this because he doesn't trust us anymore either?" Bess asked.

"I don't think so," Art said. "It's all been piling up...the kids, our new communication abilities, and our relationship with the Parmans...The Antareans have had a lock on the lion's share of trade in this galaxy. Maybe we have become too important to their plans."

"Art and Bess are right," Ben said. "Amos put his trust in us. Now, maybe, he thinks we might use our influence and abilities to somehow take over the Antarean missions."

"Maybe he thinks we will act like Earth-humans back home," Mary said. "You know...driven by greed and power hungry."

"We never gave him reason to think that of us," Ruth said.

"No, but he was on Earth long enough the last time to become aware of those qualities in our government and leaders," Ben said.

"You mean what Mersky did, or tried to do?" Ruth asked.

"Yes. And with Mersky showing up this way, I'm inclined to think he may be whispering in Amos's auditory orifice," Ben answered. "He is not to be trusted. And I agree with Ruth. We've got to see the children."

"Immediately," Ruth said. Everyone agreed. "And with Mersky," Ruth added, "let's follow Don Corleone's advice to his son, Michael in that *Godfather* movie. "Keep our friends close, but keep our enemies closer."

"Well," Bess said, smiling, "I think we're in good shape on that account."

"How's that?" Mary asked.

"We can't get much closer to him than Annabella Costa already is, now can we?" Everyone, including Panatoy, had a good laugh.

CHAPTER SEVENTEEN
GREETINGS ON PACCUM IN MANIGRA

Brigade Commander Betty Franklin heard the angelic voices of the children's choir of Saint Nicholas of Tolentine in her mind. "Do-oh-no, no-oh-bless, pa-a-chem, pax. Do-oh-oh-oh, no-oh-oh-bless, pa-a-a-a-chem." She had grown up, Felicity Mary McKensey, in a Roman Catholic enclave in The Bronx. Her nickname was "Betty" because her mother thought she looked like Lauren Bacall whose nickname was "Betty."

The Catholic Church was the center of her life in her formative years. She attended Catholic school, from kindergarten through twelfth grade, and mass every Sunday. Then she met Murray Franklin, a neighborhood boy. They fell in love. Much to the chagrin of her family, her priest, and many friends, she converted to Judaism and married Murray.

After years of traveling the Galaxy, visiting many planets and meeting so many different beings, any organized religion, especially those espousing theirs as the "true religion," seemed parochial and primitive to her. She witnessed the glory of creation everywhere, not just on Earth and understood that with the development of cognitive life in a peaceful, civilized society, there was no place, or reason, for divisive and bigoted religion. It was clear that on Earth, religion was nothing more than a scam, perpetrated mostly by old men, to control others, especially women.

At this moment, as she was about to step onto a planet in another galaxy, having been greeted in her native tongue by someone who knew the children of Butterfly House, Betty Franklin felt uplifted and privileged. She was at one with the Universe. She sensed being a part of the endless space around her; galaxies beyond galaxies that seemed to have no boundary; no containment; no beginning; no end. How far she had traveled from that church in the Bronx...how far she still had to go. Yet it was not strange. She belonged here.

"Do-oh-no, no-oh-bless, pa-a-chem, pax," sang in Betty's mind again. "Grant us peace," she uttered as she led her Brigade landing party out of the Probeship, onto the dull gray, clay soil of Manigra-Sparkle-Plenty-Paccum-Prima-Quad-twenty-four.

The planet's blue dwarf sun tinted the bleak landscape pale violet. Atmospheric sensing equipment indicated an oxygen-nitrogen atmosphere with the presence of a few of the more exotic gases, xenon and argon, which were rare on Earth. Betty told her crew to keep their breathing devices on. A healthy variety of vegetation spread out around them. The horizon line was measured at a distance of more than two hundred kilometers, indicating the size of Paccum to be more than twice that of Earth. Its gravity was tolerable. There was a strong indication of water present, although none could be seen from their landing area. There were no beings to greet them.

Betty's second in command, Francis Rush, scanned the area, sending data and images up to the Mothership in orbit above them.

"I have no air-breathing life forms on the scope," Rush told his commander. Betty strained, listening for the voice she had heard on their approach to the planet, but there was only silence.

"What is your life-scan setting?" she asked Rush, who had been a mortgage broker during his life on Earth. When given the possibility of various jobs in the Brigade, he chose life sciences, a field that had always fascinated him in his youth, but one that he never pursued. He jokingly referred to it as an excellent second career choice.

"Humanoid. Air breathing. Carbon based," Rush answered. Betty was about to suggest a change in the setting when she noticed something move, low to the ground in the tall, thick, elephant-grass type vegetation to her left. Rush saw it too, and pointed his scanner, which was networked with the on-board Finder. "Nothing," he told Betty as he watched the instrument's data screen.

"Switch to another setting."

"But with this atmosphere and water, and the Finder's locater program, I think we should keep..."

"Water-breather. Reptilian," Betty said firmly. "Do it now, Francis! Please." Rush made the adjustment. His screen lit up.

"Holy, Mother of God!" he exclaimed. "We're surrounded." Betty signaled for the landing party to stand fast. She stepped forward alone and signaled the universal gesture of peace—arms outstretched, palms up, head bowed.

"Welcome, Commander Betty Franklin." It was the same female voice that had communicated telepathically when they had approached the planet. "You may remove your breathing devices. You will find our atmosphere fairly compatible to your home-planet, Earth." The source of the voice moved out of the grass. It was undoubtedly a reptilian being with round, dinner-plate sized, amber scales and a round head that was proportionately large for its body. It stood on four stout legs, a quadruped with three tentacles protruding from behind its head. It was low to the ground, measuring four feet.

Betty removed her helmet and turned off her oxygen supply. The air was breathable with a pleasant odor like a rich, earthy loam. Betty signed the greeting again. In response, the being fanned its tentacles above its head and bowed.

"We are so very thrilled to welcome you, Commander Betty Franklin. You are the first visitors to Paccum."

"Thank you," Betty answered. She lowered her arms and faced the being. It turned its head slightly, so that one of its round blue eyes, positioned on the side of its head like an herbivore, viewed her directly.

"We are Aicha, a race that you might call reptilian. We are carbon based, evolved to survive and procreate using the energy from our blue sun. As you can see, that is at the ultraviolet end of the spectrum." The Aicha indicated the flora around them, as several more Aicha stepped forward. Intermingled with them were smaller Aicha, obviously the young. Their bodies had only a few scales and were covered with pale blue, downy hair. Their eyes were darker than the adults' and their nostrils much larger. "Almost all of the cognitive life on Paccum is reptilian, or I should say was, until our offspring, incubating in their eggs, began to communicate with your children on Earth. As you can see, they are evolving."

Betty Franklin was stunned by the news of this contact and the physical difference that the Aicha young displayed from their parents. She had picked up pieces of the messages from Joe Finley and Frank Hankinson, but had not yet captured the full text. Both made reference to the children and evolutionary leaps. But none had mentioned any pre-birth contact. Communication to another galaxy? What had the children done? And how?

As if the Aicha female standing before her could read her mind, it stepped forward and emitted an extremely pleasing scent that calmed Betty and the rest of the landing party. Betty relaxed and smiled.

"That's very nice," she said.

"A welcome gift, Betty Franklin" the Aicha said. "In your language, you may call me Halo. If you and your party will follow us, there are many who wish to meet you and talk about the children."

CHAPTER EIGHTEEN
TWO MISSIONS LAUNCH

While the Brigade's mission to test the children on Earth, and Amos Bright's ambassadorial mission to Klane were being prepared, most of the Brigade on Antares was saying their goodbyes and returning to their galactic assignments. The Antarean spaceport, located one kilometer below the planet's frozen surface, was a bee-hive of activity. Every available Mothership and Watership had been brought to Antares and parked in orbit around the ice planet. As their destinations were vectored and passenger manifests completed, they glided down to the floor of an ancient volcano, now frozen, and into the wide shaft that was the entrance to the spaceport. Once settled, they shut down all propulsion. They were mounted on conveyors that brought them down to the spaceport where they took on supplies, supplemented crews and boarded their Brigade passengers. Once the loading process was complete, the missions were logged into the main Antarean computers. All vehicles were launched through a second shaft in the volcano, straight up and out into space.

All but two ships were ion-drive propelled. The exceptions were two new inter-galactic Motherships, fitted with Parman drives and special navigation systems. They were to go to Earth and Klane as their shake-down missions.

Several Brigade members remained on Antares to be trained for future inter-galactic missions. They would be launched as soon as data from the current missions to the Bezzolentine and Manigra Galaxies could be analyzed, and the crews debriefed. Three more new Motherships, now under construction, were to be available shortly, bringing the total fleet to seven. With Commander Bernie Lewis on Earth, and using the remaining nine Brigade commanders in space for communication, it meant that only seven inter-galactic missions could be mounted at one time, leaving one commander on Antares as receiver.

Amos Bright's ambassadorial mission to Klane had the highest priority. The commander of his vessel was an experienced Antarean male named Subrala, who had served with Bright as a junior officer on several missions during the past four millennia. The crew was entirely Antarean, with the exception of Brigade Commander Art Perlman, who would serve as on-board communicator, as agreed, and two Parman guides, whose starlight absorption would power the space craft at supra-light speed to a nearly immediate arrival on Klane.

The complete message from Joe Finley to Bernie Lewis had now been received. It went into the details of the Sloor emergence, their contact with the Amatos and Finleys, the Sloor's knowledge of the Butterfly House children, and the remarkable evolutionary leap the Sloor race had made.

Ben Green and Ruth Charnofsky delivered the complete text to Head Counsel Spooner, in her private rooms. Ruth had asked Ben, who did the final compilation of the message, to withhold the fact that Joe's communication was for Bernie Lewis, and not the Antareans.

"If what Commander Finley says is true," Spooner told Ruth and Ben, "then the children have interfered with our basic directives regarding first contact. I also fear they have, in some inexplicable way, meddled in the evolution of a species. That, as you know, is The Master's work, and strictly forbidden."

"Until we understand what actual involvement the children had in this," Ruth told Spooner, "I think it best to delay judgment of them."

"And the Sloor," Ben added. "Remember they seem to be enamored of the children and quite grateful." Spooner abruptly stood. Such a quick move was not usual for the tall, slim Antareans whose center of gravity was rather high. She was obviously upset, and fought to control her balance.

"Meddling is meddling. These are children. They are out of control and dangerous. I will not have it! I have given instructions to Ambassador

Bright to asess the situation with the Sloor as quickly as possible. I want Commander Bess Perlman available, and at my side, to receive the report that will be communicated by her husband."

"As you wish, Head Counsel Spooner," was all Ruth Charnofsky said. She bowed politely, as did Ben, and they left Spooner's quarters without another word.

Once in their own quarters, Ruth telepathed to Ben. She blocked outside reception. "They will be watching the two of us. Ask Mary to send a message to Arthur once the Klane mission is launched. He is to direct any communication to us on Earth first, and wait for my instructions before sending anything on to Bess for Spooner and the High Council."

"Spooner will expect that," Ben suggested.

"Absolutely. But unless they can process Gideon Mersky up to commander, they cannot possibly know for sure."

"So that will force their hand."

"Yes. They will process him as soon as we leave." Ben Green was troubled.

"How do we circumvent that?"

"Annabella Costa."

"And if she can't control him?"

"Then my guess is that the children can," Ruth answered solemnly.

Within two hours of Amos Bright's departure for Klane, the Earth mission was ready to go. It, too, was using a new inter-galactic Mothership, equipped with Parmans. The journey would be made at supra-light speed, allowing an almost immediate arrival.

Ruth Charnofsky said farewell to her mate Panatoy, who was returning to be with their daughter on Subax, in Rigal Quad-4.

"Give her love from me," she told Panatoy as he embraced her. She beckoned the tall Subaxian to bend down. Ruth then kissed him and whispered in his ample ear. "Ask Autumn if she communicated with the children recently. She may be reticent and evasive. Tell her it is of extreme importance that I know as soon as possible. She can contact me directly. And, of course, tell her I love her." Panatoy stood up to his full height.

"We will both miss you, my love. Hurry home."

Several minutes later, the huge new Mothership with her Parman Guides in place, launched out of the secondary shaft into the ink-black vacuum of space. Ben and Mary Green, Ruth Charnofsky, and the delighted parents of the children of Butterfly House, felt their usual adrenaline rush at departure heightened by the anticipation of seeing and embracing the children of Butterfly House.

CHAPTER NINETEEN
REUNITED

It was the height of the hurricane season in South Florida. A week earlier, a deep low trough had developed off the coast of Africa and was now swirling through the South Atlantic, picking up energy, speed and moisture while its center tightened into a classic hurricane eye. Now at force four, it was taking dead aim on the Cayman Islands, and was predicted to make landfall on Cayman Brac in nine hours. The tiny island was already experiencing gusty winds and drenching rain showers.

Butterfly House, situated on a cliff overlooking a sheltered horseshoe shaped bay, faced due east. If the hurricane's track remained true, its eye would pass to the east of the bay, meaning it would bear the brunt of the storm. But Butterfly House was well built and reinforced with concrete walls and heavy tile roofing. It had weathered several large hurricanes over the past sixteen years.

Scott Green, the Erhardt twins, Melody Messina and Beam Amato, were meeting with Bernie Lewis in a glass enclosed sun room that faced the horseshoe bay cove. Bernie had received a message from Ben Green earlier that the mission to Earth was preparing to leave Antares. The group settled into comfortable, cushioned wicker chairs around a wicker glass-topped table. Bernie noticed a sparkle of excitement in the children's eyes, confirming to him that they knew the mission would be arriving soon.

"They have Parman Guides," Bernie said to start the meeting. The children smiled and nodded. "I know you can send and receive messages as we do, so we can drop pretenses. Using the new Mothership and

Parmans as a shakedown cruise, their voyage here will be close to real-time...but you know that already, don't you?"

"Yes, Uncle Bernie," Scott said. Bernie smiled and waited, sensing that it was time to get everyone on the same page regarding the children's plans. "And we want to tell you the rest," Scott continued, "so that you can smooth the way for our departure." His tone of voice, and assured manner, left no doubt in Bernie's mind that Scott Green was the leader of the group.

"Thank you, kids," was all Bernie said. But he was relieved. Melody Messina, who grew more beautiful every day, leaned across the table and placed her hand on top of Bernie's.

"We never thought to try to fool you or be evasive, Uncle Bernie. But there were things we had to figure out ourselves."

"And do ourselves," Joshua Erhardt said.

"For good reasons," Eric added. Bernie nodded, and placed his other hand on top of Melody's.

"I never doubted anything you kids ever did. I assumed you had good reasons. You're all very special, not just to me and your parents, but to the Brigade. As you've grown, I've watched you struggle to under-stand your powers. Now I, the other commanders, your parents, and the Brigade trust you have found your way, and will fulfill your promise. You make us all very proud."

"Thank you," Scott said for all of them. "We are what we are because of the decisions all of you made." There was a moment of great love that passed from the children of Butterfly House to Bernie, the other Brigade commanders, the parents and through them, to the entire Brigade scattered across the Universe.

"The Mothership will be here within the hour," Bernie said as he and Melody parted hands. They can come in close to Butterfly House. The storm will cover their approach and landing. The Probeship will shuttle them here. Aunt Rose is manning it now."

"We will leave Earth," Beam Amato told her mentor and protector. "But there are a few things we must do before then."

"Yes. You'll need to be tested," Bernie said.

"That won't be necessary," Scott responded. "We are quite capable of space travel."

"In many ways," Melody added, grinning. A gust of wind blew some palm fronds against the glass roof of the sun room. She and the others then proceeded to tell Bernie about the Sloor, the Achia, the Liastans and several other contacts they had made, and how that had been accomplished.

The Mothership, commanded by Antarean Ayal Mark, engaged the Parman Guide the moment they were free of Antares's gravitational pull. The Guide focused on Sun, the star of Earth's system, and began to absorb its light and energy. Within moments, the sleek spaceship surpassed light-speed to supra-light speed and moved through light-time toward its target, the blue, oxygen/water planet—third out from Sun.

Annabella Costa languidly stretched her svelte naked body under the pale-blue, down comforter. She thoroughly enjoyed the sensation of her well-toned muscles and the tingle of adrenaline as it coursed down her back and into her groin.

"You are one evil, ever-lovin' tiger," she said as she turned toward Gideon Mersky's side of the bed. But he was not there. She sat up and glanced at the wing chair where his clothes had been thrown in disarray. They were still there. Then she heard the shower running. "Cleanin' up without me, are you?" she muttered to herself as she slipped out of bed.

Mersky was shaving in the steamy shower stall without a mirror. It was something he had learned to do during his ten years as an officer in the army. He shaved by feel, but it required some concentration, so he was surprised when he felt Annabelle's soapy hand slide down his back. By now, he knew her touch and leaned back into it.

"A little lower," he said softly.

"I'll go as low-down as y'all want and need, Lover-boy."

"Sounds like a fine plan," he said, turning around to face her. He set aside the razor and embraced his shower partner forcefully.

"Oh, Gideon," Annabella whispered as he pulled her against his wet, soapy flesh. "You are such a beast!"

Amos Bright arrived on Klane with little fanfare. Most of the Brigade and Antareans there were busy with the Sloor, who had all returned from their mating flight and joined the juveniles and new born on the beach. Only Antarean Commander Beam, and Joe and Alma Finley, greeted the High Council Ambassador as he disembarked from the Mothership.

"We are honored to see you, Ambassador Bright," Beam said as she bowed while extending her hands to the side, palms up. The Finleys' greeting was quite different. Joe shook Bright's slender right hand and gently pulled him in for a shoulder-to-shoulder bump. Then Alma reached up and cupped his pale,

Modigliani-like face, gently pulling it down to hers where she planted a sincere kiss on the cheek of her old friend.

"We have missed you, Amos," she said.

"A lot," Joe added.

Bright was awkwardly embarrassed, as he always was when Earth-humans expressed their affection openly.

"Yes," he mustered. "Yes. It has been a long time and so much has happened to us all. How I envy you being able to travel and work...and now, the universe is open to us. It is a wondrous time, is it not?"

"Fabulous," Joe Finley answered.

"We can't wait to go ourselves," Alma added. Then a familiar voice shouted a greeting, as Art Perlman stepped from the Mothership and joined the group.

"You guys missed one hell of a gathering," he told the Finleys as he embraced his old friends and fellow commanders.

"So we hear," Alma said. "How is Bess? Where is she?"

"Bess is wonderful. She sends her love. She stayed on Antares for uh," Art made a quick nod toward Amos Bright, "for communication purposes. I'm here for that too."

"But you didn't have to come for that. We've been handling it from here," Joe said.

"The High Council required Mr. and Mrs. Perlman's services during our journey," Bright interrupted. "You see, it was a shakedown trip for the new Mothership and there were, uh, two new Parman Guides." His manner was abrupt; his tone defensive. That was very unlike Amos Bright. An uncomfortable silence followed for a moment.

"Ambassador Bright," Beam said, breaking the mood, "we must go to the Sloor as quickly as possible. They have gathered to meet you and welcome you to Klane."

"Then we must not keep them waiting," Bright said, indicating that Commander Beam lead the way.

The stabilizers on the Earth-bound Mothership worked beautifully, keeping the huge craft on course as it descended through the hurricane toward Cayman Brac. Alya Mark was experienced, having piloted and commanded several of the older generations of Motherships, Waterships, and transports through all manner of storms and solar winds throughout the galaxy. This new generation of inter-galactic Mothership was designed with superior handling and stability. Its ion-drive guided the huge craft effortlessly through the hurricane's powerful, swirling winds.

The Mothership entered the roiling waters of the Caribbean one mile from the eastern shore of Cayman Brac. Alya Mark guided her craft down to a depth of three hundred feet, slightly above the sea floor, then turned her heading toward the horseshoe cove below Butterfly House, and waited.

The children, Bernie Lewis, the Margolin and the Martindale families stood impatiently on the beach below the steep cliffs. The storm was growing in intensity.

"They've parked a mile out on the sea floor," Bernie shouted above the howling wind.

"There," Scott Green yelled as he pointed to a light emerging from the water to their right.

"It's the Probeship," Bernie said. "Rose has them!"

Head Counsel Spooner was furious when the guard she had sent to fetch Gideon Mersky returned to her quarters without him.

"He is with the Costa female, Head Counsel," the nervous guard told her. "Her quarters are locked. She would not answer my call."

"You may go," Spooner said with a wave of her hand. She then focused her telepathic powers onto Mersky. Before calling to him, she did something very un-Antarean. She locked onto his senses— an ancient power she had perfected during her priestly training. Such intrusion was forbidden by law, especially involving off-planet species and beings. What she experienced was confusing because she had, at that moment, stumbled upon the physical and emotional sensations of Earth-human lovemaking. Although it disturbed something very deep within her psyche, it was also intriguing and, if an Antarean can be titillated, she was. She then probed the same sensation center of Annabella Costa and found a very different emotion at play. Initially, Spooner thought it might be a male/female difference. But then she realized that while Mersky was sincerely immersed in what the Earth-humans called passion and love, Annabella Costa was not. She was play-acting, faking her emotions in an outward manner. Was this to somehow fool or control Gideon Mersky, Spooner wondered? The High Counsel withdrew her probe. "This Costa is a devious female," Spooner said aloud. She summoned the guard to her rooms again.

"Go to the Brigade female's quarters. They will come now. Bring them both to me." Spooner then telepathed an urgent message to Gideon Mersky and Annabella Costa, interrupting their showery tryst. She demand their immediate presence.

As their parents exited the Probeship, the children raced through the hurricane's wind and rain, across the wet, sandy beach, to greet them. There were shouts of joy, hugs, kisses, and tears. Eight of the children, including Beam Amato, whose parents were on missions, and thus unable to be there, stood back and enjoyed the reunion through the emotions of their peers. They were not jealous. They knew their day of reunion was close at hand.

Ben Green could not get over how his son Scott was the spitting image of his namesake, the son lost in the Vietnam War, nearly a half-century ago. Although he was only sixteen, he appeared to be the twenty years that the first Scott Green had reached before his death. When Ben released his embrace of his son, Mary Green grabbed Scott. She could not control her emotions. She hugged, and wept, and laughed, and kissed Scott's face, trying to make up for the sixteen years of absent, physical motherly love. It was an uncontrollable release of seeing the reincarnation of her dead son. Scott, the stoic leader of the children, melted in his mother's arms and also wept for joy.

Julia and Vincent Messina, Melody's parents, did not recognize their grown daughter. They had prepared an image of a young girl. The adult who ran into their arms was far from that. They were stunned by her beauty and grace.

"You are a woman," Julia tearfully told her daughter. She stroked her face. "Such a beautiful woman!" Melody also wept joyfully in her parent's embrace.

While the children reunited with the parents they had not seen for sixteen years, Bernie greeted Ruth Charnofsky with a huge bear hug.

"Still strong as an ox, Bernie," she said as he released her. She kissed him on both cheeks—a greeting she had learned in Poland, before some of her family fled from Nazi tyranny. The rest died in Auschwitz, including two brothers and her mother. It was a memory she kept alive. "Rose looks wonderful. We are so delighted to see that your remaining here did not, uh, well…"

"Make us old again?" Bernie said. "Not a day, Ruth. Not an hour."

"That means if the children aren't able to travel yet, their parents can stay here and…"

"Ruth, my dear leader," Bernie interrupted. "I don't think any of the kids will be staying here…even the Martindales'."

"But they have an infant, don't they?"

"Yes, well…you've got to meet her. The children have been working their magic on her, too." Bernie then noticed that Rose was leading the Antarean technicians and Commander Alya Mark onto the beach. A strong gust nearly blew the tall Antareans over. "The hurricane is picking up steam," he told Ruth. "I suggest we all move inside."

CHAPTER TWENTY
A WELCOME ON LIAST

As the Liastan day progressed, the reddish rays from their giant sun, which the visitors had named Musial, grew brighter and whiter so that it soon resembled Earth at mid-summer dusk. The transport that brought them to the Liast city could pass for a small eighteen-wheeler on Earth, except it had no wheels. It floated above a waterway, a canal that served as its road.

Tellic, the Liastan who first had spoken to Frank Hankinson, was concerned that the Liastan vehicle was too small for the visitors.

"The children told us of your size. I apologize for any discomfort."

"This transport is the largest we have," Shinner added.

"There is no need to apologize," Frank told them. "We are quite comfortable, and appreciate your thoughtfulness." He bent over a little and glanced out of the window that ran the length of the vehicle. "Liast is a beautiful planet."

"Thank you," Tellic said. "In many ways it is like Earth. Our air, water and soil are very similar, as are many planets in the systems we now know about. Planets in galaxies of similar age, seem to follow that pattern, or so the children say."

"We are both beings fortunate to have such planets. Ah, look," Shinner said, pointing to structures about a mile in the distance. "There. Our home lies just ahead."

The Liastan city was neat and organized. Its structures were designed for the diminutive beings that inhabited them. As they passed through the streets, it was clear that the Brigade landing party would barely be able to enter them. Frank wondered where they would stay.

The vehicle arrived at a large structure that Frank later discovered was used for visitors larger than the Liastans. The vehicle parked, settling gently to the ground. Once they had all disembarked, the gates opened. There was an upwelling of applause as Frank led his Brigade landing party into a huge, open circular arena. They were completely surrounded by rows and rows of Liastans, who were standing and applauding in welcome. The Brigade party acknowledged the greeting with waves and universal signs of friendship. They observed that although most of the seats were packed with Liastans, the rows closer to the arena's lush, grassy field, held several other beings, five different races that were also standing and welcoming the landing party. In the center of the field, a group of Liastans, and representatives of the other races, stood on a platform, applauding.

"As you can observe, Commander Hankinson, you are all most welcome here," Shinner, the city leader, said as they approached the center platform. Frank, and the rest of the Brigade party, stopped in front of the platform and made the universal sign of peace and friendship. The beings in the group returned the welcome. Two uttered soft chants. Another changed color and flicked its impossibly long tongue in the air. A tiny crystalline figure expanded to twice his size. All the gestures and attitudes clearly communicated a greeting.

Special chairs, larger than the others, had been placed on the platform for the Brigade party. Tellic guided them to their seats. Frank noted he was the tallest being present. When they reached their seats, nine Liastan children, one third the size of Tellic and Shinner, approached with bouquets of fragrant, dazzling, blue and white flowers that they presented to the Brigade visitors.

"I feel like Gulliver," Frank whispered to Matthew Cummings, his second in command. Matthew had been a Miami detective in Florida, where he became involved with investigating the strange behavior of a group of seniors. Eventually, the investigation led him, and his partner, Coolridge Betters, to the Antareans and the problems with their cocooned army. Cummings, along with Betters, and Betters's wife, Paige, had been invited to join the Brigade after they helped the seniors keep the Antarean visit a secret.

"I hear that," Cummings said. "I can handle Lilliputians, Boss. I only hope they aren't hiding any giants around."

The party was seated and Shinner stepped forward. The crowd was immediately silent and attentive. Although no microphone or amplifying device was visible, his voice was clearly heard by all.

"I will speak in the tongue of our visitors, in the manner that their children have taught us." He turned to the Brigade party. "We welcome you to Liast. We welcome you to our system that you have named Auerbach. We welcome you to our galaxy that you have named Bezzolentine. And our other visitors, gathered here today from our galaxy, and others beyond, also give their personal welcome. Ambassadors Trannis and Maliotre from the planet Moghes in the nearby Bant system..."

Two humanoids in shape and design, but with a very dark green, bark-like skin and two sets of eyes, one on the side of the head and one in front, stood and emitted a sweet, soft howl of appreciation.

"Regent Chilo, from the Hydran Galaxy, the system Pentole, the planet Karfi."

A reptilian quadruped rapidly flicked its long orange tongue in the air from side to side as its scaly skin flashed every color of the rainbow. It sang its welcome, "Hachi, hachi, sssstton, hachi. Lo!"

"Our good friend Sem-Chem, chief of the Perinoola from the Narftilo Galaxy, the Corolil System, the beautiful crystal planet, Xomin."

The tiny crystalline creature, bowed to Shinner and to the audience that surrounded them, and grew to three times its size. Sem-Chem was popular on Liast and drew a great round of applause. It swelled even more before returning to its place.

"And finally, Ambassador Pochongilolto, who has visited Earth. She is from your galaxy in the Alphard System, the planet Billont."

A humanoid that looked strikingly like the so-called aliens described in the Roswell "crash." She was a little taller than the Liastans, with translucent, blue-gray skin, no apparent ears or nostrils, a small slash of a mouth and huge, wrap-around black eyes that did not blink. She folded her delicate hands and bowed, much as a Hindu might, in greeting.

"We of Liast, who have chosen not to travel in space, are always delighted to have visitors from other worlds and galaxies," Shinner continued. "But to have the parents of the children of Butterfly House come to us is indeed, a great honor."

As Shinner continued his welcoming speech, it was monitored by Duartone, aboard the Mothership. He was frustrated and upset that no Antarean was present at the event. With Commander Hankinson engaged on Liast's surface, Duartone had no way to contact High Counsel Spooner, to inform her of this major breach of protocol.

"This is highly irregular," Duartone told Andrea Hankinson, who was monitoring the events at the arena with him.

She saw Duartone was upset. "I agree," she told him, feigning sympathy. "At times like this, I wish I had become a commander." Deep inside, she felt great pride in having the Brigade, and not Antareans, chosen to be welcomed to the Bezzolentine Galaxy by the first beings to be encountered there. Duartone turned away from the view-screen. Andrea observed that Shinner had finished his remarks. "Look, Commander Duartone," she said, "they have asked Frank to speak."

"But an Antarean must be the first to welcome," Duartone said plaintively. "It has always been that way. That is my mission. I have failed."

"You have not failed, Commander Duartone. The Liastans want it this way. It is their planet. It is their choice."

"They said the children of Butterfly House were here."

"Yes. Our children."

"But that is impossible! How can they have traveled from our galaxy?" Duartone knew of Amos Bright's missions to Earth. There were rumors of special newborn Earth-humans left behind, but nothing specific was ever revealed. All Duartone knew was that for reasons beyond his control, he had lost command of this historic mission, and Earth-human children, from a place called Butterfly House, were somehow responsible.

"Thank you for your very warm welcome to Liast," Frank Hankinson began. "This is our first visit to your galaxy. As I gather you know, I am from the planet Earth in the galaxy we call Milky Way. I informed

Tellic and Shinner that I am not the leader of this mission." Duartone listened with interest. "Antarean Commander Duartone, who now orbits your beautiful planet, is in charge," Hankinson continued. "The Antareans are a great race of travelers, educators, diplomats and traders. I am sure you will welcome them and allow their ambassador to greet you on their behalf as friends." There was a great round of applause with everyone standing and clapping, including those on the platform. Duartone felt a little better. "But for now," Frank went on, "on behalf of my mission commander, the Antarean Duartone, I greet you and offer you the friendship and the inter-galactic facilities of the Antarean race." He made the Universal sign of peace, extending his arms out, palms up and bowing.

Three-hundred sixty-eight nautical miles above the arena, Duartone's shiny, pale blue skin turned an angry yellow.

"How dare he speak and greet on my behalf without authority," the Antarean commander said. "The Master forbids it! Inform your husband that upon his return he will communicate this breach to the High Council. He stormed out of the communication center. Andrea Hankinson quickly telepathed down to her husband, warning him about what had just transpired.

CHAPTER TWENTY-ONE
FIRST VISITORS TO PACCUM

Halfway across the universe, the Brigade landing party on the planet Paccum, in the Manigra Galaxy, had been made comfortable in a single story building set into a hillside above a tranquil lake whose water was the deepest blue Betty Franklin had ever seen. It was made so by light from the blue dwarf star, now registered as Sparkle Plenty in the Mothership's Finder. Betty, and her second in command, Francis Rush, sat with Halo, sipping a tea that was both relaxing and invigorating.

"The only visitors we ever had on Paccum, before you arrived, were the children," Halo said.

"We knew nothing of their visit," Betty responded.

"They are your children, are they not?" Halo asked.

"Yes. But to the best of our knowledge, they have no way to travel from Earth into space. Our mission is one of only two to ever travel outside of our own galaxy." Halo turned to three of her Aicha companions. They communicated rapidly to one another. The sounds they made, as they waved their tentacles, were incomprehensible to Betty and Francis, even with their universal translators. When Betty tried to tune into the Aicha's thoughts, they too were cloaked in the strange language.

"The children first came to us through our unborn," Halo began. "We did not know what was happening until they hatched and we discovered that they were different."

"How were they different, if we may ask?" Francis Rush inquired.

"They were larger, especially their brains and nervous systems. And there were indications of evolving from reptilian to mammalian. Perhaps you observed this when we first met."

"The downy hair?" Betty asked.

"Yes. And warmer blood. Yet they are still adapted to our blue star you called...I forgot."

"Sparkle Plenty," Betty answered.

"Sparkle Plenty. Yes. Very poetic. We call it Pa-Ha-Cho. The life-giver. The children say the life-giver is young compared to your star, Sun."

"It will be so registered in our data banks," Francis said. "Thank you. So you see, until our young matured a little, we were not sure what had happened. We feared a disease or terrible mutation. Then they began to tell us about the children of Butterfly House and what they had learned from them while in egg. It was most extraordinary!"

"The children taught your young before they were born?" Betty asked, surprised. She knew there had been an indication that the children communicated with each other while in-utero, but to have the ability to reach across galaxies to unborn was mind-boggling to the Brigade commander.

"Yes," Halo answered. "And afterward, the brain capacity of our young more than doubled. Through them, your children began to teach all of us."

"Teach? Teach what, may we ask?" Betty inquired.

"To join with all life in the Universe. They told us why we, the Achia, would be able to join, while there are many who cannot." Halo's words were confusing. What did "joining all life mean?" And why were the children espousing this?

"What, may we ask, makes one kind of being able to join with all universal life while another cannot?" Betty asked Halo. The Achia leader poured more tea.

"Those who war cannot join; those who enslave; those who defile the environment; those who take not for need, but for greed; and those who believe they alone are chosen by a supreme being to rule over others. Those who do all this in the name of a god, master, lord, maker, omnipotent ruler...They cannot join the Universe of peace."

Like Commander Duartone orbiting Liast, in the Bezzolentine Galaxy, Antarean Commander Shai-Noa, now orbiting Paccum in the Manigra Galaxy, was very upset and annoyed at not being invited to the planet's surface to invoke a proper Antarean greeting and welcome. She tried to listen in on the conversation that Commander Franklin and Francis Rush were having with the Aicha, but was blocked. Commander Shai-Noa's frustration was increased by the fact that her only means of communication back to the High Council and Spooner was through Betty Franklin. "This is unacceptable," she said aloud. The Parman Guide, who was resting while the other was on duty on the Mothership's hull, overheard Shai-Noa's complaint. It passed the information on to its companion. Both vowed to tell Betty Franklin as soon as they had the opportunity.

CHAPTER TWENTY-TWO
A DIRECT ORDER

Spooner was upset. She had an uneasy sensation that developments on Earth, Klane and in the two galaxies they were now exploring, were slipping out of her hands. Was the relationship between the Brigade and the Parmans subverting Antarean control? Had she proceeded with inter-galactic travel too quickly? Had the Antarean High Council been careless in integrating the Earth-humans into The Master's Grand Plan?

These troubling questions weighed on her mind as she waited for her guard to bring Mersky and the Costa woman to her. The Parmans were a critical key to inter-galactic travel. Discovering them, and their unique ability to absorb star light, had opened the Universe to Antares eons ahead of any engineering breakthroughs that might have occurred. Yes, discovering the Parmans must be part of The Master's Grand Plan. And was it coincidental that the old Earth-humans ingratiated themselves with Amos Bright, and thus were processed and brought to Antares? Surely their presence to replace the earthbound, cocooned Antarean army was no coincidence. That too must be part of The Master's Grand Plan. It had all seemed so right, so positive, especially when the ten Brigade commanders had developed the ability to communicate instantly across the vastness of the Universe. To Spooner, that now seemed a troubling, double-edged sword. Immediate messaging was critical to inter-galactic travel, but it put the Antareans' inter-galactic fortunes at the mercy of the Brigade. How could she, her commanders, and the High Council, be certain that the content of their messages was accurately and securely forwarded?

And then there were the Brigade births. These children at Butterfly House, and their abilities, were also troubling. What had the Master created there?

After Gideon's and Annabella's in-the-shower lovemaking had been rudely interrupted by Spooner's telepathic summons, they dressed hurriedly. The guard Spooner had sent to escort them stood stoically at the outer door to Annabella's bedroom. Once they were ready, the tall Antarean, carrying a ten-foot spear-like weapon, took them directly to Spooner. He walked behind them and did not speak. When they arrived at Spooner's quarters, he opened the door and gestured for his charges to enter.

"Sorry to disturb your activities," Spooner said coldly. There was a hint of sarcasm in her voice—something very un-Antarean. "There are matters to be addressed immediately." Her tone of voice was formal and sharp.

Annabella, who sensed that Spooner had taken some delight in interrupting their tryst, blocked her own thoughts and was wary. Mersky, who had introduced Annabella to Spooner at the gathering, was nervous. He, too, sensed the hostility in Spooner's demeanor.

"We are here only to serve, Head Counsel Spooner," Annabella said, bowing slightly.

"Your summons was no problem, Ma'am," Mersky added.

"Antares has need of you both," Spooner continued, ignoring the politeness of her visitors. She turned her attention to Annabella. "Seek out Commander Bess Perlman. Tell her that I require her services, and bring her to me." It was a strange request in that Spooner could have summoned Bess Perlman herself by guard or telepathically.

"Of course, Head Counsel. I will go to her quarters immediately," Annabella said. But before leaving, she gave Mersky a tender kiss on his lips. Although her mind was blocked, she knew that the kiss would disturb Spooner. Annabella smiled to herself and left.

"You and Miss Costa are quite friendly," Spooner said after Annabella closed the door behind her.

"Yes. I suppose so," Mersky responded, trying to seem nonchalant. "The processing and all this..."

"Yes. Yes. Of course," Spooner said, dismissing his explanation with a wave of her long, thin hand. The priestly tattoo on her arm showed for a brief moment. Mersky took note, unaware of its significance. "Sit down, Mr. Mersky." It was more an order than an invitation. He found a bench and sat. Spooner glided across the room, placing her seven-foot frame next to him. He craned his neck to keep eye contact as she towered over him. "As you may know," she began, "our primary directive is to spread the word and Grand Plan of our Master. We Antareans, who for millennia have moved among the stars and planets of our galaxy, are now, by the grace of The Master, expanding this great work to other galaxies."

"It is a marvel," Mersky said, respectfully.

"More, Mr. Mersky. It is a holy mission." It was the first time that Mersky had heard any reference to holiness in space. On their way back to quarters from his mini-tour of the Great Hall of Kinnear, Amos Bright had made reference to some of the history of Antares and priestly orders that once ruled. But he had seen no evidence of organized worship or priests.

"The Master has provided us with the Parmans," Spooner continued, "whose guidance and energy absorption allows us to escape our galaxy in real-time, supra-light speed. This inspired our engineers to built wonderful new Motherships." Spooner's pride caused her pale skin to glow. "The Master has also given us the Brigade and its commanders." Mersky wondered where she was she going with this, and why she was telling him as a matter of urgency. "Their telepathic communicative abilities make instant, inter-galactic communication possible." Spooner was no longer looking down at Mersky. Her gaze was somewhere else, hundreds of millions of light years across the void of deep-space. "These gifts from The Master will now extend our reach and knowledge to the very boundaries of the Universe. The possibilities for Antares are infinite…" Spooner paused. "Yes…infinite," she repeated as she returned her focus on Mersky. "You will become a Brigade commander today. But you will not travel into space. You will stay here to be my personal aide, my personal communicator." Her words were an order, and because Mersky was new to Antares, he had no idea how out of character such an order was for an Antarean to make to another species.

Being an ex-military man, Mersky understood when an order was being given. Amos Bright had explained the process of becoming a commander and the enhanced powers it would give. But Bright had spoken in the context of Mersky joining the Geriatric Brigade. There had been no mention of exclusive service to Head Counsel Spooner.

"Our technicians are preparing to begin your processing," Spooner said. She silently signaled for her guard, who immediately appeared. "My guard will take you to them." There was finality in her voice.

Mersky followed the guard, his heart pounding with excitement as he contemplated the new powers he would have and how they could bring him closer to his goal of bringing some, or all, of the children to Earth for himself and his partners to exploit.

Shortly after Mersky's departure, Annabella Costa and Commander Bess Perlman arrived at Spooner's quarters.

"Where has my Gideon gone to?" Annabella asked, stressing the word "my".

"On an errand for me, Miss Costa," Spooner answered smoothly. Annabella was about to ask what errand, but Spooner abruptly turned her full attention to Bess Perlman, effectively dismissing Annabella. "Commander Perlman, I need you to send a message immediately." Bess bowed her head respectfully.

"Of course, Head Counsel Spooner. I am here to serve."

Spooner probed Bess's mind, searching for a clue to her loyalty and sincerity. But she was blocked. "We have given these commanders far too much power," Spooner thought to herself, also blocking. She then contemplated invoking her priestly powers to break through Bess's wall of privacy, but thought better of it. That would reveal too much. Better to save that surprise for another time, or critical situation.

"The message is for Ambassador Bright, on Klane."

"Shall I write it down?" Bess asked.

"Not necessary," Spooner answered. "Just say that at my order, Gideon Mersky will process to commander today. Once he is established, all communication to and from me will channel through Commander

Mersky. He will be on my personal staff." Bess had been prepared for this action, but was surprised at the speed with which Spooner was moving.

"I was under the impression, from the High Council meeting, that we Brigade commanders would have the opportunity to discuss this matter."

"There is no longer time for that," Spooner said with a wave of her hand. This time Bess took note of the strange tattoo on Spooner's arm. "Just send the message. And have your mate forward it to my Mothership Commanders in the Bezzolentine and Manigra Galaxies via Commander Hankinson and Commander Franklin. Is that clear?"

"Yes, Head Counsel Spooner," Bess answered. "What you have ordered is clear. But I must inform you that this is not what the Brigade expected." Bess's tone was firm, but respectful.

Spooner moved with cat-like stealth, gliding across the translucent floor, very close to Bess. She reached down and put her hand firmly on Bess's shoulder, then bent down and positioned her long, oval face directly in front of Bess's.

"Let me be clear about this, Commander Bess Perlman. I order this message be directed only to those I have specified. It is not to be sent to any other Brigade commander. Be sure to give Hankinson, Franklin and your mate, Arthur, the same instructions. Do you understand?" Spooner's attitude made it clear that any further argument was futile.

"I hear what you say, Head Counsel Spooner. You are aware that these messages can be captured by any Brigade commander."

"I am aware your communications remain suspended in space and time, and thus, they can be retrieved. But unless a commander is notified, he or she will not look to find it. Once Gideon Mersky has been processed, he will be able to tell me what you sent, and where you sent it. Is that clear? Do we understand each other, Commander Bess Perlman?"

"Very clear, Head Counsel Spooner," Bess responded as she gently removed Spooner's hand from her shoulder. "Since this is a priority, I require concentration without distraction. Please excuse me. I will return to my quarters to do your bidding."

Annabella Costa, who had quietly stood aside, took Bess's hand in a show of sisterly solidarity. They left the room together. Once a safe distance from Spooner's quarters, Bess guided Annabella into an alcove in the hallway. They both blocked any outside mind-probing.

"We can't stop them from processing Mersky to commander," Bess said. "Time is of the essence. He is in your charge now. Be aware that although his powers will be greatly increased, he will not immediately understand how to engage them. Perhaps we can delay." Annabella smiled and patted Bess's hand.

"Darlin'," she said, "where I came from, and what I know about men and their appetites...well, let me assure you that Gideon Mersky's, or Commander Gideon Mersky's powers are no match for mine between the sheets."

CHAPTER TWENTY-THREE
AN URGENT MESSAGE

The children, Alya Mark, the Antarean technicians, Ruth Charnofsky, Ben and Mary Green, Bernie and Rose Lewis and the Martindales were all gathered in the large solarium on the southern side of Butterfly House. The parents were being given a tour of the facility by the Margolins.

The children were unmovable in their determination not to be tested by the Antarean technicians. Commander Alya Mark was just as adamant, stating that she would not allow any of them aboard the Mothership unless they were tested. But, she assured them that if they were found to be capable of deep-space travel, they would be processed and welcomed.

The all-glass enclosure held exotic tropical plants, many in full bloom. Their fragrance permeated the tense atmosphere. Outside, the hurricane hammered the small island. Sheets of rain splattered on the thick, curved glass roof, gathering and forming rivulets that poured down the sturdy glass sides and onto the patio.

"Those are my orders," Alya Mark said firmly. "I cannot disobey the directive of the High Council and Head Counsel Spooner. And my Mothership is needed back on Antares soon."

Having stated the case as strongly as any loyal Antarean could, the Antarean Commander bowed her seven-foot frame to the children and awaited their response. The children, who had listened to Alya Mark politely, showed no sign of concurring, disagreeing or arguing. They sat in silence.

"I think the commander has made a good case for proceeding," Bernie Lewis finally said. "Testing will be done quickly. You've told me that you are sure you are ready for space travel. Well then, that's good news. This will just be a confirmation...a formality. Then we can all get on with the business of packing up and leaving Butterfly House. What do you say, kids?"

There was a long pause in which all the commanders in the room, Brigade and Antarean, tried to read the children's thoughts. But they were blocked. Finally, Scott Green, the group's leader, stepped forward and addressed the visitors.

"Commander Alya Mark, we appreciate your loyalty to your leaders and to your mission. If you are saying that unless we submit to your technicians testing us, you will not take us to Antares, we can only respond by wishing you a safe voyage home." Ben Green, who had been quietly sitting with his wife, Mary, in the rear of the room, could not contain himself. He leaped to his feet.

"Look here, Scott. Now listen to me! Nothing's gained by being stubborn, and I must point out, also rude to our Antarean friends. Everyone here knows that without them many of us would be either discarded old folks waiting here for the grim reaper, or would have already met him. And you guys would not exist." He looked at the other commanders present, who nodded their agreement. "So how about acting like adults," he continued, "and getting on with it so we can all get out of here and back to the good work we were doing? You have no idea what a glorious life awaits you all."

Again there was a long, awkward moment as the children blocked their thoughts and emotions from outsiders. Scott focused on his peers. It was obvious that they were holding a rapid, complex discussion telepathically. Eyes flicked from one to the other. Once, then twice, they all looked at Melody Messina, then the Erhardt twins, then Scott.

While this was happening, Ruth Charnofsky sensed an urgent message coming from Bess Perlman. She got up and stepped outside the glass room, into an ample potting shed where gardening tools, special soil and seeds were stored.

"Hello, Ruth," the message began, "I have been ordered by Head Counsel Spooner to communicate the following message." Ruth cleared her mind and opened herself to reception. Bess's voice sounded disturbed. "Gideon Mersky is being processed to commander immediately. He is not to be in the Brigade. Repeat, not in the Brigade. He will be her personal communicator." Ruth now knew that Spooner had a growing fear that Antarean reliance on the Parmans and Brigade for inter-galactic communication put too much power in their hands. "I have been ordered," Bess continued, "to send this message immediately and exclusively to Arthur, on Klane, to Frank in the Bezzolentine Galaxy, and to Betty in the Manigra Galaxy." The idea of exclusivity disturbed Ruth. Divide and conquer. There was more. "To clarify, so there is no mistake, I am ordered to tell Arthur, Frank and Betty to relay this only to their Antarean commanders. I have been given strict instructions not to, repeat, not to, deliver it to you, or the other Brigade commanders. Spooner knows that unless notified, messages are not readily received. Please advise as to what you wish me to do, as soon as possible. Mersky will be able to pick up this message once he learns how to channel his powers. I have no doubt he will report my disobedience to Spooner." The message ended.

"We must respond," Ruth muttered aloud to herself. "Spooner has thrown down the gauntlet." But how? They were too far away, and too involved on Earth to get back to Antares before Mersky became a commander.

Inside the sun room, Scott Green faced his father. This was a confrontation he did not want, but Ben Green's attitude left him little choice.

"We all want to get out of here, Dad," Scott began. "But there are things that you just don't understand..."

"I understand stubborn adolescents when I see them," Ben told Scott. "I haven't been away from Earth that long." Scott smiled and shook his head.

"It's not what you think, Dad. So much has happened..."

"This will all have to wait," Ruth announced as she strode briskly into the room. "Right now, I need to meet privately with Ben, Mary and Bernie."

"I think I can save us all a lot of time, Aunt Ruth," Scott said as she reached his side, "and trouble." He signaled for Melody Messina to join him in front of the group. As she came forward, Scott asked Beam Amato to bring the Brigade parents to the solarium, as well as the Margolin family.

At the same time, Bess Perlman began her transmission of Spooner's message to Klane, Liast and Paccum. Also, at that moment in time, the rain and wind suddenly stopped and the sky began to show patches of blue. Sunlight illuminated the glass-enclosed room. The eye of the hurricane was passing over Butterfly House.

CHAPTER TWENTY-FOUR
REVELATION AND PROJECTION

It took several minutes for the Brigade parents and the Margolin's to find seats and settle down in the solarium. The eye of the hurricane had moved by swiftly, and Cayman Brac was now experiencing the fiercer back end of the storm. Ruth had questioned Scott about what he meant by "saving a lot of time," but the young man politely asked her to be patient.

"There are things happening that need my immediate attention," she chided him. "Your father was correct. We have no time for adolescent games." Scott smiled calmly, frustrating her even further.

"We are just as concerned as you are about Gideon Mersky becoming a commander. I promise you we will address that situation first." Ruth realized that Scott, and most likely the rest of the children, intercepted the message that Bess had just sent.

"You're saying that you can receive Brigade commanders' messages?" she whispered, not wanting Alya Mark to overhear.

"Yes, Aunt Ruth. We developed that communication ability long before you realized your own." He glanced away for a moment, noting that everyone in the room was settled. Ruth was awed by that revelation. "And there is much, much more to be revealed...some now, some in good time, Aunt Ruth."

Scott signaled for Melody Messina to join him in the front of the room. He gestured for Ruth to take Melody's seat. The rest of the children were seated with their parents. The Martindale family, and the Margolins were settled in the front row of wicker chairs. Everyone was quiet. Even the precocious six-month old, Carmella Margolin, was attentive. The storm's fury increased outside, hammering the glass roof of the sun room with sharp staccato rhythms. Scott stepped forward.

"On behalf of the children of Butterfly House, I want to welcome all of you: Antarean Commander Alya Mark, Brigade Chief Commander Ruth Charnofsky, my parents, Brigade Commanders Ben and Mary Green, the Antarean technicians and, of course, all the reunited Brigade families. Welcome!" There was a burst of applause. Scott smiled and nodded. "It's great to see you all." He waited for the room to settle, which was helped by a loud clap of thunder. "Even Kate agrees. That's the name of this fortuitous hurricane." Scott's light attitude changed. He stepped closer to his audience and lowered his voice. He glanced around the room, finally settling on Commander Alya Mark and the Antarean technicians. "We understand your anxiety to be on your way back to Antares, and how you might think our refusal to be tested as being obstructive, adolescent petulance. I can assure you that is not the case. We, too, are anxious to leave Butterfly House. It has been our home, our only home. Now it is time for us to move on. We have much to do in the Universe." As he spoke, he gestured above to the dark, stormy clouds that raced by above the glass enclosure, depositing a downpour of hard, wind-driven rain. "I can also assure you that we are more than able to travel, as you will see shortly." He turned toward Ruth and his father. "We are not petulant adolescents. For the past three years we have traveled Earth, learning, meeting people and observing life on this planet, our birthplace. Long before we were conceived, here is where our genetic makeup was first created by the Antarean's processing. We have observed the man-made artificial borders. Each side calls the other alien. But you all know that among space travelers and those civilizations aware that our Universe teems with life, nothing...no one is alien. None with that knowledge make war, as they do on Earth. The races out there are not, as Earth-humans depict, mindless, highly advanced beasts, intent on destruction or conquest. Quite the contrary. Those who travel in our galaxy do so peacefully and respectfully. We have seen this through your eyes, and in other ways."

Many of the Brigade members in the audience nodded their agreement. Ben Green saw his son in a new and different light. He had, until now, pictured Scott as a sixteen-year-old teenager. But the man he saw speaking before the group was far more mature and poised. He exuded charisma that held everyone's attention.

"Before leaving our home planet," Scott continued, "we needed to understand our roots. That's why we spent the past three years away from Butterfly House. We saw that bigotry, hatred, egotism and avaricious power might destroy humanity on this planet; perhaps even the planet itself. Earth-humans can't seem to be able to live peacefully with one another or respect differences. Religion, race, creed, ethnicity, language, nationalism, greed, poverty, feudalism, monarchy...it is, compared to the Brigade, Antareans, and the other space travelers, primitive. There is no place for such ignorance and arrogance out there." Again he gestured to the storm above. "Do you know, not long ago, they fired a rocket to explode on what they called, 'just a comet'? It destroyed an entire crystalline life form—a thriving civilization. They have exported the genocide they practice here. The Parmans were furious, but have kept their anger to themselves. They know the Brigade was not responsible. Earth-humans have much to learn and change if they are to survive. But clearly, they are not ready to join the Universe."

"Is there no way for you to help your fellow Earth-humans?" Julia Messina, Melody's mother, called out.

"We cannot remain here, Mother," Melody answered. "But we contacted certain children in many lands, while they were still in the womb. We taught them and expanded their abilities. They were born with intellect and powers far beyond any now on Earth. They are evolved beyond their time. They telepath with one another. They already have many common goals—to end war, terrorism, despoliation of the environment...Their abilities and knowledge will grow. It is possible that they will find a way to save this fair planet if others will listen."

"Could you not remain here and help them, Scott Green?" Alya Mark asked.

"No, Commander, we cannot. We knew, before our birth, that your processing our parents to travel in space had set off a series of genetic alterations. Those changes made us a new humanoid race. We are no longer like our peers on Earth. We are no longer like our parents. We are evolved beyond them."

Ruth was focused on Scott with great interest. But at the same time, she worried about Gideon Mersky's transformation into Spooner's personal Earth-human commander. Many of the powers Scott was discussing would pass on to him. Precious time was passing. Bess was on Antares, waiting for instructions. As these thoughts raced through her mind, a familiar voice spoke to her.

"Please don't be anxious, Mother," the voice whispered. It was her daughter, Autumn, telepathing from Subax! She was with Panatoy!

"Autumn?" Ruth messaged back. "You can hear? You have these powers, too?"

"We all do, Mother. Trust us. Listen to Scott. My friends there will show you marvelous things. I will see you soon." Ruth noticed that Melody Messina was smiling at her and nodding. Scott was finished. He stepped back, next to Melody.

The children and their parents stood and applauded. Alya Mark was not sure that what the young man had said altered her orders. But she was made uneasy by the power the young man had shown.

Ruth and Alya Mark both stood up to speak at the same time. Scott raised his hand to silence the group. "Please, just wait a little longer, Aunt Ruth and Commander Mark. Melody and I now have some pressing business that will affect us all." His voice was polite, but as persuasive as any commander, Antarean or Brigade. Ruth and Alya Mark sat down. The audience was again silent.

Scott took Melody's left hand in his right. The two then spread out their free hands and arched their backs so that they were looking straight up at the glass roof and the storm above. The room grew dark and a circle of light surrounded the two. It widened as a space, but did not include the others in the room. That space began to fill in with another place, much like a holograph in which the two children were the centerpiece. And then the place became clearer. It was the private quarters of Head Counsel Spooner, on Antares.

Those in the solarium watched in awe, as an audience might in a theater, where the curtain had been raised to reveal a stunningly surprising set. Scott and Melody had somehow projected themselves across the galaxy. It had to be an image. Yet their presence in the solarium and in Spooner's quarters, was simultaneous and real.

CHAPTER TWENTY-FIVE
CONFRONTATION ON ANTARES

"What is this?" Spooner demanded, as Scott and Melody materialized in front of her worktable. "Who let you in here? Guard!" she shouted. But no guard appeared. "Who are you? Guard!" Scott bowed deferentially.

"He cannot hear you," he told Spooner.

"We are, Head Counsel Spooner, in a dimension outside of his," Melody said, also bowing respectfully.

"I am Scott Green, son of Brigade Commanders Mary and Ben Green."

"And I am Melody Messina, daughter of Brigade members Julia and Vincent Messina. They were recently here for the gathering, but are now on Earth," Melody told Spooner. She then extended her hand in friendship. Spooner stood, leaned her long body over the table, and grasped Melody's hand.

"You are two of the children of Butterfly House, are you not?"

"We are," Scott said. "We are here and there. The mission you sent to Earth, led by Commander Alya Mark, is able to see and hear us."

"See and hear? But how is this possible?" Spooner asked.

"It is possible," Scott responded, "for the simple reason that we are able. That is the best answer I can give you. We are here for one specific purpose. When we return to Antares with our parents, we will reveal more."

"That response is unacceptable," Spooner told the two children. She was not used to being put off when she asked a question.

"What is unacceptable, Head Counsel Spooner, with all due respect, is that you have ordered the processing of Gideon Mersky to be your personal Earth-human commander," Scott told her politely, but firmly.

"We are here to ask you to immediately rescind your order for his transformation," Melody added. Spooner stiffened to her maximum height and glared down at Scott and Melody.

"I will overlook your arrogance as that of badly reared Earth-human children. I do not know how you can appear before me, but I will not tolerate your uninvited presence any longer." She made a motion to move toward the door of her quarters, but found she was unable. "Release me!" Spooner demanded.

"You are within our projection," Scott told her. "Leaving it can only happen when we leave. All we ask is that you cancel Gideon Mersky's processing to commander status."

"That will not happen, Child," Spooner said, folding her long thin arms across her chest in a defiant pose. As she did, the mark of her priestly station was revealed.

"You are of a priestly order?" Scott asked.

"That is not your concern, Child," Spooner said, covering the ancient glyph with her sleeve.

"Then you no longer do The Master's work?" he asked. Spooner became very angry—an emotion rarely exhibited by an Antarean. Her pale skin turned milky white. Her eyes widened and her mouth curled inward, until it nearly disappeared.

"How dare you question my devotion to The Master and His glorious plan. How dare you! Your parents know, the entire Brigade, the galaxy knows Antareans serve The Master."

"Yes," Melody said. "But it appears that you have lost sight of His glorious plan."

"Nonsense," Spooner answered. "Childish nonsense."

"Has it not occurred to you that journeying to Earth, establishing a base there millennia ago, returning for your cocooned army, meeting and processing our parents and the others that became the Brigade, is all The Master's work?"

"Everything is The Master's work," Spooner muttered with a wave of her hand. Her mouth began to widen and some of her pale blue pigmentation returned.

"Yes," Scott said. "Including the ability we and our parents have to communicate across this galaxy and beyond. We, the children of Butterfly House, are a new generation, a new race...a race you helped create. Is this all not part of The Master's plan? Have you lost sight of it because your ego will not accept our role in it?" Spooner was taken aback by Scott's lecturing her. But his words gave her pause. What hidden powers did these children possess? Were they, perhaps, messengers from The Master?

"What is that role?" asked Spooner. Her tone was calmer and friendlier.

"At this moment, it is to advise you, Head Counsel Spooner, that giving Gideon Mersky Earth-human commander powers will cause you and Antares great difficulty."

"And why is that?"

"Mr. Mersky once held a powerful and critical post in the government of our parents' nation on Earth," Scott explained. "He controlled great military forces and used his position to make wars in which many Earth-humans perished. The secret purpose of those wars was to gain power and wealth for himself and a group of his associates on government and business."

Back on Earth, in the solarium, Ruth thrilled at Scott's and Melody's confrontation with the powerful Antarean leader. She glanced over at Alya Mark and the Antarean technicians. They were riveted in place, and also quite pale, not from anger, but from fear.

"When we were born, he tried to keep us captive on Earth to serve these selfish purposes," Melody continued. "But he did not understand our powers, and those of our parents. He still believes that we all left Earth. He knows nothing of Butterfly House."

"Yes. I know that. And now we will test to see if you can travel. What does it matter if Mersky knows or does not know? He is here among us now."

"What you do not know," Melody told Spooner, "is that Gideon Mersky never gave up his plan to have us back on Earth, there to do his bidding. He, and his greedy friends, plan to use us to give them wealth and power."

"He waited until he reached the right age," Scott continued, "remembering the promise that Amos Bright had made. When contacted, he was ready to be processed and brought to Antares. But what you do not know is that before he left Earth, he made plans with his associates to use his power and position to bring us to Earth. Of course, as you know, he never knew we were there all the time."

Spooner was now more than curious. Doubt began to gnaw at her. It was true that she did not like the power the Brigade commanders had by being her sole source of inter-galactic communication, or their close friendship with the Parmans. But she silently had to admit to herself that she still trusted them. What these wondrous children were now revealing about Mersky was disturbing. Was he playing her for a fool?

"If what you say is true, I want to hear it from Mr. Mersky, himself."

"Excellent," Scott said. "You may call your guards now to bring him here."

"And Bess Perlman too," Melody suggested.

Everyone in the solarium sat in silence. They watched Spooner order her guards to cancel Gideon Mersky's processing and to bring him and Commander Bess Perlman to her quarters.

While she watched Scott and Melody wait with Spooner, Ruth quietly told the Greens, and Bernie Lewis, about Bess's message.

"I think you should tell Bess what has happened," Ben suggested.

"I will. This projection the kids can do is really something!" Ruth said, grinning.

"Incredible," Ben added. "I had an idea about some of this," Bernie Lewis told the others, "but not to the extent we're seeing. I think it's wonderful."

"Yes," Ruth said. "And my guess is that we have not begun to know what it all means." She then left the room for a few moments, to message Bess, on Antares. The message got through just before the guards arrived to bring her to Spooner's quarters.

"I will not stand here and be accused by these children," Mersky announced angrily, after Spooner had questioned him about the plans he made with his associates on Earth.

"Then you deny what they say is true?" Spooner asked. "You did not make plans to bring the children back to Earth to serve your self interests?"

"I certainly did not," Mersky answered emphatically. "I was invited here by Counsel Amos Bright. I chose to come to serve Antares. How could these Brigade children possibly know anything about me? They were infants when they left Earth." Head Counsel Spooner stretched to her full height, a sure sign that she was angry.

"Were you not going to use their blood to make vaccines; use their powers to spy on others; use their knowledge to gain power, Mr. Mersky?" Spooner pointed her long, tapered index finger as she spoke. Her words were not questions, but accusations.

"Absolutely not!" he declared. His voice wavered a bit.

"May we speak to Mr. Mersky, Head Counsel Spooner?" Scott asked.

"Of course." She lowered her hand. Both Scott and Melody moved closer to the ex-Secretary of Defense.

"Do you know where we live?" Scott asked. Mersky folded his arms and stared at the two young people contemptuously.

"I haven't the slightest idea. I saw you all leave on those three shuttles sixteen years ago, and have heard nothing more until Jack Fischer contacted me on behalf of Amos Bright who invited me to join the Brigade."

"We have been living on Earth, Mr. Mersky," Melody said softly.

"All but three of us," Scott added. "They live on their fathers' planets." Mersky frowned, uneasy and confused.

"I saw you leave with your parents."

"You saw three shuttles leave. What you didn't see was the Probeship return," Bess told Mersky. "We, and the Antareans, did not want to chance taking our babies into space. And we did not want to risk their safety by letting you know that."

"When you were making your clandestine plans in Texas," Melody told Mersky, "we were onto you and your greedy pals. You see, Mr. Mersky, ever since you tried and failed to keep us captive when we were infants, we have watched you."

"When Commander Bright promised you could join the Brigade," Scott continued, "he was naïve about people like you and your thirst for power. His only Earthly contact was with our parents, who were all older and retired. They were just average folks who had lived long and carried within them experience, and the tolerance that age provides. That is the very reason why they are such an asset to the Antareans and The Master's Plan."

"But we knew that you came from a place of wealth and privilege," Melody continued. "You abused your trusted position. You represent the very worst of our species and planet. We are now here to make sure that you will never have the opportunity to exploit and enslave us."

"Or ruin anything else in the Universe," Scott added.

"Yes. I see now," Spooner said as she moved across the room next to Mersky. She towered over him, peering down like a parent might over a badly behaving child. "You now have a great dilemma before you, Gideon Mersky. You will not become a Brigade commander, nor remain in my presence. And with the powers you now possess, I cannot allow you to return to Earth. To add you back into that bubbling cauldron of self-tudestruction goes against our prime universal rule that forbids intentional meddling in the affairs of other species. It is clear that you, and your associates, would only encourage disaster."

Mersky was frightened. He was light years from Earth among beings he had underestimated—Antarean and Brigade. He had been duped about the children. Now he was at their mercy. Bess Perlman read his mind.

"What shall we do with you, Gideon?" she asked. Spooner spoke before he could answer.

"We must find a place for him where he cannot harm anyone, especially the children. Perhaps, in time, he might learn to be a positive part of The Master's Plan."

"What about sending him along on the next inter-galactic mission?" Scott suggested.

"Do you mean as a Brigade member?" Spooner asked.

"Not exactly. Sort of a trainee," Scott answered.

"Yes," Bess agreed. "It can be a provisional assignment. In our life in space we have time on our side. Apparently a great deal of time. Perhaps Mr. Mersky will learn what his positive place is in the Universe."

"Agreed," Spooner said. "And to be sure he is kept on that course, I suggest Annabella Costa be assigned to the mission." Bess smiled at Spooner's insight into Earth-human behavior.

"I believe she has an innate ability to, shall we say, hold Mr. Mersky and his emotions in check," Spooner concluded.

Bess departed with Mersky and a guard to find Annabella Costa, leaving Spooner and the two children alone.

"Thank you, Head Counsel Spooner," Scott said. "I hope you can now see that testing us for space travel is not necessary."

"That is quite obvious, young man. Can Commander Alya Mark see me?"

"Yes," Melody answered.

"Alya Mark, you are relieved of your orders to test the children of Butterfly House. They, and all others, shall be transported back to Antares as quickly as possible. Use your Parman Guides. Notify us when you depart." When Spooner finished giving the order, she turned back to thank Scott and Melody for their service to The Master, but they were gone.

CHAPTER TWENTY-SIX
IN THE GENES

The holograph of Spooner's quarters that the audience on Cayman Brac observed faded until all that was left were the images of Melody and Scott. The darkness that surrounded them also faded and the front of the solarium returned. Scott's and Melody's presence was totally back on Earth. As everyone applauded, the commanders and parents were on their feet, firing questions at Scott and Melody.

"How did you do that, Melody?" Julia Messina asked.

"Do you project yourselves physically, or is it just an image?" Mary Green wanted to know.

"How long ago did you learn to do this?" Bernie Lewis inquired.

"Are you able to teach this method of travel?" Alya Mark asked.

"Why didn't you visit us this way?" Stuart Erhardt's father asked.

"Where else have you traveled this way?" Ruth asked as she walked briskly to the front of the room. She had just received another message from Bess Perlman, reporting the appearance of the two children and the cancellation of Mersky's processing to commander. Bess had asked Ruth if she should forward any of Spooner's messages. Ruth told her to wait.

"To answer you first, Aunt Ruth," Scott began, "we have projected to many places. Planets, asteroids, moons, comets...We have met wonderful beings out there."

"Klane?" she asked. "The Sloor?"

"One of our first projections. They are our very good friends," Melody acknowledged.

"But you never came to us this way. Why?"

"We spoke to you telepathically," he answered. "And there was much to do before we were ready to reveal this ability." His response did not satisfy Ruth or the rest of the Brigade parents present. Ben Green stood up.

"What did you have to do that was more important than being with your parents?" His deep voice had a tremor of anger in it. Several parents in the room joined him, asking their children the same question. The voices in the room grew loud and dissonant. The children were surprised at their parents' reaction. Although they were a new race and advanced beyond many in the Universe, they were still young in many ways.

Bernie Lewis, who among the Brigade commanders knew the children best, stood up and whistled loudly. Everyone was startled and fell silent.

"Okay, everyone. Let's calm down and get a grip. The last thing we need, after all these years, is confrontation and argument. I am not as surprised as you about the ability that Scott and Melody have shown us. I've lived with your kids for sixteen years now. They are gifted and powerful; special in every sense of the word. But they are also just wonderful kids; caring, hopeful, energetic and possessing an untainted and with an original outlook of their place in the Universe. I think they know all about us, and our lives...who we were, and weren't, before the Antareans gave us our rebirth. Bottom line? I trust them. I suggest we all do the same."

Bernie's common sense calmed the atmosphere in the room. It gave the Brigade parents and the commanders pause. Then Beam Amato stood up and walked to the front of the sun room to join Scott and her close friend, Melody.

"Thank you, Uncle Bernie," Beam said. "We did not desire to hide anything from you all, or the Antareans. But first we had to understand these phenomena ourselves."

"It was one thing to learn how different we were from our peers on Earth," Scott added, "and quite another to know how different we were universally." He turned to Alya Mark, who had been patiently waiting for an answer to her question.

"Forgive me, Commander, for not answering you directly regarding our ability to teach others to project. The short answer is simply, no." The Antarean showed her disappointment by lowering her head and slightly lifting her narrow shoulders in a shrug.

"That is most unfortunate, Scott Green," she said softly. "The Master instructs that all technology is to be shared."

"What you have seen here is not technology. It is an ability of our unique genetic makeup. As we confirmed to Head Counsel Spooner, it was you, the Antareans, who began the great change that brought us into the Universe. You processed our parents and changed their genetic makeup. From that event, we were conceived and born. Our ability to project cannot be taught but perhaps it might evolve in another race. Only time will tell. As long as Antares procreates by cloning, genetic advancement will depend on science and technology to make those decisions. You now create duplicates that possess memory and characteristics of the hosts. You no longer mix your genetic pool, and therefore avoid accidental combinations that can cause defects. But it is through those same accidents that evolutionary leaps occur."

"I understand," was all Alya Mark said, but her thoughts, which she did not block, reflected her questioning of basic Antarean society. She silently expressed her vow to bring the matter of changing their reproductive processes before the Antarean High Council.

While Scott spoke to Alya Mark, Ruth Charnofsky observed Melody and Beam deep in conversation. She tried to listen in, but was blocked.

"Will you tell us about the Sloor, Melody?" Ruth asked. "We have heard that there have been some remarkable evolutionary changes on Klane. You said they were your very good friends." Melody shot a quick glance at Scott. He nodded back to her.

"We can do more than that, Aunt Ruth," Melody said. She took Beam Amato's hand and stepped forward. "Rather than tell you, if you will all clear this area, Beam and I will show you." As everyone moved back, the storm outside seemed to lessen. The thick clouds, still gray and rain-laden were not rushing by as fast. The sky brightened a bit, while the room began to darken. Another projection was underway.

CHAPTER TWENTY-SEVEN
A VISIT TO KLANE

Once again, the front of the solarium became a stage. The physical area around Melody and Beam faded to black, but they remained clear and in place. Then a red glow began to grow around them. It was the atmosphere of Klane, tinted by its giant red star. Rock formations materialized in the foreground and behind the two children. The gray, oily sea of Klane became visible in the distance. Thousands of Sloor, adults and juveniles, were gathered on the shore of the sea.

Melody and Beam walked to where the Antarean Ambassador, Amos Bright, was addressing the Sloor. His long, thin, pale-blue arms, protruding from his sheer, golden ambassadorial robes, were visible though his transparent protective suit. Bright's hands were held high, palms up, fingers apart and pointed outward in the universal sign of greeting and non-aggression. His face was partially hidden by his breathing device and translator.

"Our purpose in coming to your planet is one of peace. Our wish is to develop a bond of friendship; to share our knowledge of the Universe; to invite you to share with us, and other beings, in the bounty of The Master's creation." It was the official greeting that Antareans had pronounced throughout their galaxy for millennia upon millennia.

The Sloor leader, the same adult male who had first contacted the Finleys, stepped forward in front of the thousands of his kind. He bowed and spread his magnificent wings to their forty-foot span. His metallic feathers sparkled in the red Klanian sunlight. As he lifted his head to respond to Amos Bright's greeting, he saw Melody and Beam walking toward him. The giant Sloor turned from Bright and bowed again, this time to the children who, unlike the other visitors to Klane, wore no protective clothing, breathing devices or translators.

"Greetings," the Sloor leader said. "Here are our good friends. Welcome Miss Melody Messina and Miss Beam Amato. A most glorious and long-awaited welcome!" He bowed his head again until his beak touched the ground and his wings lay flat on the beach in a submissive pose.

"Beam?" Marie Amato shouted. "My darling Beam?" She ran from her place in the group behind Amos Bright, toward the two girls. Because she had not seen Beam for sixteen years, she halted momentarily, wondering which of the beautiful young women her daughter was. Her question was answered as Beam ran to her mother. They tearfully embraced. Beam's father, Paul Amato, was right behind his wife, joining the embrace by wrapping his arms, encumbered by his protective suit, around Marie and Beam. To the great pleasure of the Brigade onlookers on Klane, and in the Butterfly House sun room, the Amato family was reunited. Melody then approached the Sloor leader.

"It is so very good to see you, Machoi," she said. Up to this point, no Sloor had revealed a name to the visitors. "I bring greetings from all the children of Butterfly House. They hope to visit with you again, soon."

"That will be a great honor, Miss Beam Amato. And now you must come and see what you have done," he said, sweeping one great wing aside and gesturing to the Sloor gathered behind him on the beach. "As you predicted, we are becoming."

Melody looked beyond Machoi's wing to the gathering of Sloor. She noted that the young now had black feathers in place of scales. And they were air breathing through holes in their iridescent skin, where gills had once been. Yes! They were changing from amphibian to avian, much like the birds of Earth evolved from dinosaurs. But, unlike the millions of years it took on Earth, the transformation of the Sloor occurred within one generation.

"Look what has happened to our young while still in egg," Machoi said proudly. "We are so grateful."

"Becoming, is the way of the Universe," Melody assured him.

"No!" Amos Bright proclaimed. "It is the way of The Master!" He walked toward Melody who was now joined by Beam and her parents. Antarean Commander Beam, Beam Amato's namesake, Brigade commanders Alma and Joe Finley and Art Perlman followed close behind the ambassador. "Everything that happens in the Universe is but a gift from The Master. This is the way of all that exists!" Bright's tone was adamant. With a graceful move of his massive plumed, beaked head, Machoi turned his attention to Amos Bright

"You may call our becoming your Master's work. Whatever name you give it matters little. We Sloor know the true source," Machoi said, dismissing Bright's claim with a slight movement of his right wing. "The children imparted this gift to our young within egg. We are part of existence; part of the Universe. Sloor, Antarean, Earth-human are all made of the same, and so we are the same, and we are becoming what we may be tomorrow, if we survive."

"Not true," Bright told Machoi and the gathering of Sloor behind him. "The children come from the Geriatric Brigade. The Brigade comes from interaction with us, the Antareans. We, who have traveled this galaxy for millennia, and now travel beyond to other galaxies, are guided by The Master and his Grand Plan."

"Very well," Machoi responded. "Then we thank you and your Master, Antarean Ambassador Bright. And we thank the Brigade people here as well...and first and foremost, the children of Butterfly House." He bowed to Amos Bright and the rest of the group. "It matters not how this advance came to us, only that it did occur, and that we assure it will continue. We are dedicated to survive. We will become." Bright bowed to Machoi. His role as ambassador, High Council and former Antarean Commander was primarily diplomatic and non-aggressive.

"We respect your beliefs. May this be the beginning of our everlasting friendship." Unsaid, Bright knew it would take a long time to bring the Sloor around to recognizing The Master. However, he was comfortable that time was on his side. It was the "teaching" by the children that disturbed him. Years of space travel as an Antarean commander had taught Amos Bright patience and diplomacy in the face of adversity and unexplained phenomenon. He would not confront this now.

The audience at Butterfly House watched the events with great interest, noting that the Antareans on Klane, notably Counsel/Ambassador Bright, had not questioned how Melody and Beam had appeared.

After the welcoming was complete, and Melody and Beam had spent personal time with the Sloor, Bright invited the two young women back to the Antarean base. The Finleys, Amatos and the other Brigade members there had many pressing questions for Melody and Beam. Amos Bright purposely kept his amazement at the girls' sudden and mysterious appearance on Klane, one that the Sloor seemed to accept without question, to himself. Back at the base, he maneuvered things so that he was alone with the girls, unaware that their journey was being viewed on Earth.

"So, you have visited the Sloor before. And now you appear again. Please tell me how you traveled here." His tone was diplomatic, polite, interested, yet demanding.

"We call it projecting," Melody answered calmly.

"How does projecting happen?"

"As I told Head Counsel Spooner earlier this day, we..."

"You were on Antares this day?" Bright asked, interrupting.

"Oh yes. We can go anywhere. We told her, Scott Green and I, that..." Once again, a confused Amos Bright interrupted.

"Scott Green? This is Ben and Mary Green's son on Earth?"

"Yes," Melody answered.

"And he spoke with Head Counsel Spooner?"

"Scott and I went to see her together," Melody said, smiling sweetly as though they had just walked around the corner to see Spooner rather than across the galaxy.

"Incredible!"

"Not really." Melody smiled. "As I was saying, we told Head Counsel Spooner that we would better explain projection and other things, when we all reached Antares on the Mothership."

"The ship that brought the mission to Earth?"

"That's correct," Beam answered. "That will happen shortly after we leave here. As far as how we project, well, it is because we have been genetically altered."

"A result of the original processing that you did to our parents," Melody added. "You started a genetic chain reaction that resulted in us—a new race with abilities we have explored."

"And continue to. That's us," Melody said, smiling, "explorers."

"And what did you do to the Sloor? The leader, Machoi, mentioned teaching their young in egg."

"We spoke to them," Beam answered.

"That is to say, we communicated with the young before their birth," Melody explained. "You know we did that with one another before our births. We taught them how to increase their mental capacity and power."

"We helped them adjust their genetic code to evolve, as they say, 'become,' more rapidly than might occur without our help," Beam added, making their involvement sound normal and logical. But to Amos Bright, it was far more complicated and disturbing. His shock grew to un-Antarean anger. His skin stretched to full height.

"Interfering in species evolution is a very serious offense among space travelers and traders."

"We did not alter or splice genes. We only spoke with them."

"No! What you have done is blasphemy." Bright towered above the girls as they sat on plush, cushioned chairs in his opulent quarters. Rare Antarean anger smoldered behind his dark, almond shaped eyes. "You two shall not return to Earth today. I will escort you to Antares. I will have Head Counsel Spooner notified immediately of this...this gross interference and law-breaking. I shall..." Melody held up her hand to silence him.

"Excuse me, dear Ambassador/Counsel Bright. Before you go any further, know these three things. First, we are being seen and heard back on Earth by the children of Butterfly House."

"Your telepathing is of no concern to me."

"Also," Melody continued, "the Brigade parents, Chief Commander Ruth Charnofsky, Commanders Bernie Lewis and Ben and Mary Green, and your own Commander Alya Mark and her technicians can hear and observe. That is part of our projecting ability." Bright was stunned. He looked around the room, a conference chamber in the guest quarters of the base, designed for the ambassador's personal use.

"I do not see anyone," he said suspiciously. But at the same time his threatening stance decreased substantially.

"But they can see you," Beam assured him.

"Second," Melody continued, "All the Brigade commanders are now aware of our presence here, and our eminent departure from Earth to Antares."

"They can all see you? Even those not on Earth?" Bright asked.

"Yes. If you attempt to detain us, then all communication between Brigade commanders in this galaxy, plus those working in Manigra and Bezzolentine, will cease."

"You threaten me? You dare threaten the High Council and The Master's work?" He paled and rose to his maximum height again. Although Antarean nature is not aggressive, they have encountered hostile beings in their travels. Almost all were, like Earth-humans, relatively primitive, so at times, the Antareans had to defend themselves, or subdue, until they could either make peace, or withdraw. Almost always, this only required an aggressive pose and the presentation of potentially overwhelming force—force that they would never use for conquest. Rarely did they have to actually engage in hostilities, and those were over quickly, with no loss of life, because Antarean weapons were designed to immobilize, never to injure or kill.

Amos Bright's aggressive pose did not frighten the girls. But then a voice inside his mind stopped him cold. It was the Sloor leader, Machoi, speaking to him telepathically.

"You are not on Antares, Ambassador/Counsel Bright. This is Klane. The children are under our protection. Be warned." Melody and Beam also heard Machoi.

"Please, Ambassador Bright," Melody said softly. "We are just informing you. We know what a good friend you have been to the Brigade...to our parents."

"And we all respect the opportunity you gave our parents by offering them a life in space," Beam added. "You had no idea you were physically tampering with a species. Like you, we mean no harm."

"On the contrary," Melody added. "You have seen how we have helped the Sloor to become. We do the same for all."

Bright was not convinced that the children's evolutionary 'help' was in the best interests of Antares, or The Master's plan. But the idea that so many were witnessing this meeting, one that he assumed would be private, made him hesitate. Now Machoi had warned him. A hostile encounter with the Sloor would not be the best start for his role as Ambassador/Counsel. Bright relaxed. His thin lips widened across his face as he tried to emulate an Earth-human smile.

"I cannot jeopardize the missions in the Bezzolentine and Manigra Galaxies. Losing communications might be disastrous." He again reduced his towering physical presence and bent his thin frame down to the girls' level. His voice was calm and measured. He bowed low and spread his arms in an apologetic pose. "I did not mean to threaten. Of course you are free to leave."

"Thank you, Ambassador Bright. We shall have more to say when we reach Antares. May we assume you will be returning soon?"

"I will pay my final respects to the Sloor, with the hope that they will accept an Antarean embassy on Klane, and depart. We travel on a new Mothership with Parman Guides."

"Then both our journeys will be in real-time. Perhaps we will both arrive on Antares today," Melody said, extending her hand in friendship. Amos took it in his. The young Earth-woman's grasp felt warm and honest.

"You said there were three things I had to know, Melody Messina."

"Yes," she answered. "I want to inform you that Gideon Mersky will not become a commander, by order from High Counsel Spooner...That is, at least not for the foreseeable future." Bright nodded his acceptance without comment. He would wait until he met with Spooner.

It was time to leave. Melody and Beam bid farewell to the Amatos, the Finleys, and the other Brigade members on Klane.

"I will see you very soon," Beam assured her parents. "Out among the stars." They hugged and kissed.

Machoi had gathered the young Sloor on the beach. They were now capable of telepathing and speaking several languages they'd learned from the children. Most of the adults had already left to forage, and to enjoy their time on land. When the temperature and acidic consistency of the gray, oily liquid changed, they would return to the depths, to bear their young and wait for the next cycle.

"We shall visit you again soon," Melody promised the young Sloor and their leader.

"At the next mating?" Machoi asked.

"Perhaps even before the next emergence," Beam told him.

"But we shall not be emerging," a young female reminded the girls. "We are now air-breathing. We will remain on the surface. Only our parents will hibernate to the depths."

Melody and Beam realized that the Sloor were now branching into two species. They wondered what the offspring of these young air-breathers would be. The girls suspected the change would be more radical than these young who were already very different from their parents.

They speculated that the new generation, born on land, might bypass gestation in egg and be born live.

There was much embracing and demonstration of affection. The young Sloor wrapped their wings around the girls and stroked their heads with their curved golden beaks. The girls then bowed, stepped back, and began to fade way from Klane.

CHAPTER TWENTY-EIGHT
VISITORS AND DEPARTURE

Melody and Beam projected their full selves to Butterfly House and received a round of applause for a job well done. Now it was time to move on—to leave Earth and begin their work. Commander Alya Mark's new orders from Spooner were to transport the children and their parents to Antares as soon as possible.

The hurricane had passed, and damage, other than to trees and some beach erosion, was minimal. Power lines on the island were down, but Butterfly House, with its two powerful generators, was electrically self-sufficient. The compound was a beehive of activity as preparations were finalized for departure. The Mothership, now six miles off shore, prepared to move closer to the cove, allowing the Probeship to deliver passengers quickly under cover of darkness.

Scott met with Ruth, his parents, Bernie and Rose and the Margolins in the solarium. Joining them was Mad Man Mazuski, still visiting on the island. He sat in as an observer as the future of Butterfly House was discussed.

"Once the word goes out that you are able to travel in space," Bernie began, "a whole mess of Brigade couples, Earth-human and mixed-mating, will start families. Butterfly House will be a busy place for a long, long time."

"That's for sure," Ruth agreed. Scott turned to the Margolins.

"You two have been so important to us. I hope you will consider staying on." Alicia Margolin looked at her husband. Phillip smiled and nodded.

"We are delighted you asked us," Alicia said.

"Nothing would make us, and our kids, happier," Phillip agreed.

"Wonderful!" Rose exclaimed.

"There's just one thing..." Phillip paused to gather his thoughts, knowing he was making a life decision. Alicia's smile encouraged her husband. "By the time we are old enough to travel in space," Phillip began, "our children will be grown with lives of their own. We know Butterfly House's mission must remain secret, but we don't want our kids to have to stay here if they don't want to. If we can work that out, then we are prepared to spend the rest of our earthly lives here..."

"What he means is that we will impatiently wait to join you in space," Alicia said, interrupting.

"If you will have us, that is," Phillip added.

"Are you kidding? You two have meant so much to us here," Ruth responded. She placed her hands on Alicia's and Phillip's shoulders. "You will be a great asset to the Brigade, and welcomed with open arms."

"Remember that we chose you from the womb to be our teachers," Scott added. "You guys are the best!"

"Thank you. All of you." Phillip was emotionally choked. "The kids... I mean they might opt to stay here and maybe take over our roles. Or they might not. Are you open to that eventuality?"

"Anything and everything is possible," Scott said. "As far as I am concerned, the answer to both your questions is yes. Am I right, Aunt Ruth?"

"Yes, Scott. We trust Alicia, Phillip, and their children to keep the secret of Butterfly House. Just as we do Mr. Mazuski, Jack Fischer, Phil Doyle, Mr. DePalmer, and President and Mrs. Teller," she said.

"And don't forget the doctors who helped us with the births," Rose added. "Although they, along with Mersky, never knew the children were here, they did keep the secret of their existence well." Everyone agreed, nodding their concurrence.

"Good," Bernie said, rubbing his hands together. "Then that's settled."

"I'll need to know what to tell them all," Mad Man said. I mean I know it's not my place to interrupt, but with you all gone and...uh..."

"Of course," Ruth said. "That's why we arranged for you to have your boat here. Soon it will become clear." Mad Man nodded and listened, wondering exactly what would "become clear."

"Did you contact Jack Fischer?" Scott asked Bernie.

"Everything is waiting on Siesta Key." He looked at his watch. "In fact, I think it's time for you to fire up the Probeship and pick them up," he told Rose. She got up and gave Bernie a kiss on his cheek.

"Trusting your wife to take it out solo?" she teased.

"My dearest," he answered, "after soloing twice to the moon and back, and picking up our visitors on this trip, I'd trust you to take it anywhere."

All through the mild, moonless tropical night, illuminated only by starlight, the children of Butterfly House moved their belongings down the steep steps to the beach. Their parents helped, excited to be a family together and on the move.

A while later, Scott and his parents gathered with the Erhardt twins and their parents, Lillian and Abe, the Margolins, Ruth, Bernie and Mad Man Mazuski on the patio. Excited sounds of activity filtered up from the beach below. They sat at the table that the Lewises, Margolin's and Martindales had breakfasted at every sunny morning for the past sixteen years. Four Tiki lamps on brass stands served as illumination.

"Rose will be back within the hour," Bernie told the group.

"Is everyone on board?" Ben asked.

"Everyone. Jack Fischer said it was a tight schedule, but they all made it."

"Good old Jack. He's been there for us since the beginning," Mary recalled. There was fondness in her voice for the Miami fishing charter captain who had been the first Earth-human to help the Antareans twenty-one years ago when Amos Bright and his crew came to retrieve their cocooned army.

"And he's kept in touch with all the families who believed why we had left, and where we all went," Bernie added.

"Jack sure did a great job helping us get out into the world," Scott added.

"So, Jack's coming here?" Mad Man asked.

"And others," Ruth told him.

"Others?"

"You'll see. It's a surprise."

"Jack and surprises. That's how we met all of you," Mad Man joked.

"Yes," Ruth said. "And someday, when you're old enough to be processed, you all might join us. But for the foreseeable future, we will need your good services, Mr. Mazuski." Mad Man shrugged and smiled.

"My pleasure," the ex-chopper pilot said.

Bernie was sitting between Ben and Mary Green. He reached over and took their hands in his. "Now...Rose and I have had sixteen wonderful years here with the children. As you can see we have not aged the way raising twenty-two children might do to unprocessed folks." Everyone laughed. "We love each and every one of them. You must be very proud that Scott has been chosen to be their leader."

"We surely are," Mary said. She smiled at her son.

"And I am delighted," Bernie went on, "that you two have volunteered to return to Butterfly House, to teach and protect the next group of our babies, which I am sure are already being conceived, light years from here."

"Absolutely," Ruth agreed. "Word has gone out that it is safe to begin families."

The announcement that the Greens would take the place of the Lewises was news to Scott and the Margolins.

"That's great," Alicia Margolin told Ben and Mary.

"Awesome," Scott added as a loud cheer rose up from the beach below.

"I gather Rose and her charges have arrived," Bernie announced.

Rose's passengers had rendezvoused on Siesta Key, on Florida's west coast. She had maneuvered her craft underwater, up a wide canal to a posh mansion. It was after midnight. The neighbors, mostly wealthy retirees, were asleep. Jack Fischer greeted her with a warm hug. The trip back to Cayman Brac was uneventful. Rose had kept the sleek, supersonic craft just a few feet above the calm Caribbean, avoiding radar and evading any boats that might cross her path. She zoomed past Cuba before its defenses could identify the Probeship as an aircraft and not an electrical anomaly. As she approached Cayman Brac, she submerged and brought the Probeship into the cove below Butterfly House. Only the front edge of the craft was exposed on the smooth, sandy beach.

As the people from the patio made their way down the steep steps to the cove, Rose led her passengers out through the Probeship's forward hatch onto the beach. First out was Malcolm Teller, ex-President of the United States, and his wife, Margo "Honey" McNeil Teller. She had been his press secretary sixteen years ago when both were enlisted to help organize safe, secure and secret locations for the births of the children. The Brigade parents and children greeted the Tellers warmly.

Next out were three doctors. First was President Fuller's medical advisor, Dr. Michelangelo Yee. Next, a former Chief of Obstetrics and Gynecology, Dr. Khawaja. Finally, a pediatric surgeon/fetal specialist from Albert Einstein Medical Center, Dr. Robert Chollup. They had been lead members of the staff at NASA Houston's Building 11. Their team had delivered the children now gathered on the beach, and the three that had been taken off-planet to the homes of their non Earth-human fathers. The doctors were amazed to see that the parents had not aged, but looked years younger. When they saw the children, knowing they were only sixteen, their maturity and physical development astounded the physicians.

Next to exit the Probeship were two old friends of Butterfly House, the Brigade and the Antareans—Jack Fischer and Phil Doyle. Both were retired Miami charter boat captains. They were greeted by their good friend, Mad Man Mazuski, who had, by then, arrived on the beach with the rest of the people from the patio.

The last to emerge was a man known only to a few as Mr. DePalmer. He was a shadowy figure, a private banker who had handled the finances and special logistics for Antarean and Brigade visits to Earth, as well as the expenses of running Butterfly House. He stood aside quietly, in suit and tie, as the other passengers from the Probeship mingled with the children and their Brigade parents and commanders.

While all this was happening, Alya Mark and her team of Antarean technicians quietly boarded the Probeship. Rose piloted them to a rendezvous with the waiting Mothership, offshore.

The reminiscences, joy and pride among everyone on the beach continued for nearly a half-hour. Excitement in the cool night air was palpable. The great accomplishment of protecting and raising this very special group of children was coming to an end. A new life for them was about to begin. Bernie Lewis quieted everyone down and motioned for them to gather around.

"Alya Mark has informed me that the Mothership is now safely parked on the dark side of the moon. They are ready to receive us. The Parman Guides are in place, eager to meet the children, and delighted that they are the ones to bring them out into the Universe." A cheer rose up from the children. It echoed off the cliffs, across the calm cove, and out to the open sea. "Before those who are leaving go on board, I have a few people to introduce and a few words to say." Another cheer, but this time the excited children were joined by their parents. Bernie gestured toward the new arrivals. "You all know Jack Fischer, Phil Doyle and Mad...uh, that is, Mr. Mazuski. They have been stalwart in their support of the children and Butterfly House." More loud applause. The three men had been meticulously careful as liaisons. They transported the children to the mainland and escorted them to the various colleges and universities they'd attended. They also kept the families of the Brigade members updated on their loved ones. The fact that these families had kept the secret of the Brigade was miraculous. Then again, talk of alien abductions and visitors from outer space was met with skepticism and scorn on Earth. No one wanted to be labeled a nut. Jack, Phil and Mad Man now had the certain knowledge that when they reached their 60s, they had an open invitation to join the Brigade.

"They are here with Mr. DePalmer," Bernie continued, "who most of you don't know." The quiet banker waved shyly to the crowd. "Mr. DePalmer handles our finances." Bernie then pointed to the three doctors. "These men knew you kids from the moment you appeared." A nice round of applause welled up.

"They are Dr. Michelangelo Yee, Dr. Shariat Khawaja and Dr. Henry Chollop." The doctors nodded and smiled. Dr. Khawaja spoke in a soft voice. Everyone strained to hear him. Even the sound of the waves gently lapping on the beach seemed to abate.

"We are so extremely pleased to see all of you so...so well. All grown and healthy, and quite beautiful. Knowing you at birth, and now understanding a little about the journey you are embarking upon, makes us proud to have been part of your lives. We wish you Inshallah, great success."

"Finally," Bernie continued, "I would like you to meet two people who had a great deal to do with getting you all born safely and secretly." He gestured toward Malcolm and Marge Teller. "We don't have the facilities to play 'Hail to the Chief,' but here are President and Mrs. Teller." Everyone applauded.

"Thank you," Malcolm Teller began. "It is thrilling to be here and see all of you, grown and vital. Have sixteen years really passed? It seems only yesterday that we visited you as infants in Houston. And now you are about to embark on what I know will be a great and wonderful adventure." The ex-president walked among the children and their parents with the same warmth and friendliness, the common touch that had endeared him to everyday people, and had won him two terms in the White House.

"On the way here, Jack Fischer and Rose Lewis informed us of your amazing progress, and some of your wonderful abilities. I wish you could all stay here on Earth and help humanity understand that we share a small, beautiful planet in an endless universe, and that we have to learn to take care of it. But I know your calling is out there." He gestured toward the starry sky. "I know you will enrich all life that you encounter. I know you will think of us and your home planet and keep us in your prayers as we will you. We wish you Godspeed and safe journey." As the applause echoed off the cliffs, President Teller and his wife continued to walk among the children and their parents, clasping hands and embracing as many as they could.

It was time to leave. Rose and Bernie said their goodbyes to Phillip, Alicia and their children. They embraced Jack Fischer, Andy Doyle, Mad Man Mazuski, and gave a warm handshake to Mr. DePalmer.

"Safe journey back to Florida on Mad Man's boat. And take good care of yourselves and Butterfly House," Bernie told them. "The next group of Brigade couples will be here before you know it to bear their young on our home-planet."

"We'll be here, Bernie," Jack Fischer told the departing commander. They had been close friends for more than twenty-one years. "And," he added, "one of these days, we're gonna be seniors, Bernie," Jack kidded. "Right, guys?"

"Oh yeah," Phil Doyle said.

"Can't come too soon," Mad Man said. "So keep a nice place ready for us out there. Okay?"

"You got it," Bernie said. "I'll personally come get you." He turned to Ruth. "Chief Commander, I think it's about time to get this show on the road."

"Just a few more Earthly matters, Bernie," Ruth said. She walked up to a higher part of the beach. Her back was against the cliffs. "I am delighted that we leave Butterfly House in such good hands. On behalf of the entire Geriatric Brigade, now scattered throughout this galaxy, and in galaxies beyond, we thank you." She was addressing the Margolins; Peter and Tern Martindale and their children Laga, Lucas and Rode, and Ben and Mary Green. All would remain as protectors, trainers, communicators and teachers for the next generation of Brigade children. "Our leaving Earth was only a first step. These wonderful children are the next. Many more will come here to be born and follow us out into the Universe. But we will remember that Earth is our home-planet; always in our hearts and thoughts." She turned to President and Margo Teller.

"The children asked me to bring you here this night because they have things to tell all of us about Earth and its future. Scott?"

As he stepped forward, so did the rest of the children, until they, as a group, faced their parents, the commanders, and those who would be staying behind. Scott was an imposing figure, dressed in the light blue Geriatric Brigade jumpsuit that all now wore. All, that is, except Joshua and Eric Erhardt and their parents.

"Before we leave to fulfill our destiny, we want you all, our parents, commanders, Earth-bound friends, and especially President and Margo Teller, who have expressed their desire for us to help this troubled planet, to know that we will always regard Earth as our home-planet too. We are not leaving it without giving it our help. During the three years that we were away from Cayman Brac, we visited every continent, every country and every people. We saw great promise, and great danger. By now, most of you know that we have also traveled to the farthest corners of our galaxy, and beyond, meeting with many beings and life forms. Yes. Our work is out there. But we could not abandon Earth to extinction—a course it is clearly set upon. And so we have planted the seed of survival in hundreds of young people all over the world. We have taught them to raise their mental capacities. They can telepath to each other, and to us. They can effect change, should the greedy fools of this world continue to degrade Earth's environment and inhabitants. They will learn to control their powers and to use them wisely. Our hope is that they will eventually guide the beings of this fair planet away from disaster."

Scott's words were a great surprise. The idea that such powers had been given to a few young Earth-humans might be construed as meddling in the evolution and destiny of a race and planet. Had the children decided to reject the code of space travelers and traders? His words troubled the parents and commanders. That emotion passed silently among them. This was neither the time nor place to confront the children. A purple glow in the east signaled the first light of morning.

"We know there are more than fifty Brigade matings, some mixed, who have already conceived in space. Many more will join them. The good people gathered here to run Butterfly House will need help. The young people we have taught will be contacted by my parents who are taking on the role that the Lewises so ably filled." Ben and Mary nodded to the applause of the group. "Joshua and Eric Erhardt, and their parents, Lillian and Abe, are also staying behind for a while, to help prepare the way for those arriving to give birth here in eight months." Scott then gave a silent signal to the children. One by one, they bid farewell to the Erhardts, Greens and the others they were leaving behind.

In a matter of fifteen minutes, the travelers had boarded the Probeship. As the first faint rays of morning turned the deep purple eastern sky deep rose, and then pink, the sleek craft rose out of the water and streaked toward a rendezvous with the Antarean Mothership parked on the dark side of the moon. Eric Erhardt was on board. He would fly the Probeship back to its hiding place on the underwater reef, offshore from Butterfly House.

CHAPTER TWENTY-NINE
COSMIC CONSIDERATIONS

The Parman Guides transported the Mothership from Earth to Antares in real-time. It took a mere two Earth-hours from the time the passengers from the Probeship boarded on the far side of Earth's moon, to the moment they were welcomed by Head Counsel Spooner, at the Antarean sub-surface spaceport. She personally welcomed each of the children in the unprecedented manner of taking their hands with both of hers and bowing. Part of her action was a genuine welcome. And part of it was to see if she might sense something about the children by making physical contact. But the children blocked her, showing her nothing but a warm greeting, respect for her position, and their gratitude for bringing their parents out into the Universe.

The Earth atmospheres and 24-hour cycles from the gathering were kept in place for the visitors' comfort. While the children and their parents settled into their quarters, Ruth and Scott met with Gideon Mersky and Annabella Costa in the apartment the lovers now shared. Nothing of the future of Butterfly House, or the anticipated arrival in nine months of a new crop of Brigade children, was discussed. Although the children had foiled Mersky's attempt to become a commander, Ruth still did not trust Mersky. He would have to prove himself. Now, by his demeanor and tone of voice, she knew she had made the right decision.

"No matter what you two think you can do," Mersky told Ruth and Scott in a strong, defiant voice, "I am here. I am processed and as capable as any Brigade member. I won't go away. And I am not bound to any arrangement you have made with the Antareans."

"There is no arrangement, Mr. Mersky," Ruth told him. "We serve with the Antareans by their invitation and our choice. You are a guest here, as are we, far from Earth, in an environment that assures your survival and nothing more. You have been given a gift. What you now make of the long life ahead of you is your choice alone."

"And if I choose to return to Earth?"

"We will not transport you, and neither will the Antareans," Scott said. He was not as concerned about Mersky.

"And if by chance you get someone else to take you," Ruth added, "be assured that your fellow Texas conspirators will turn on you. They will see you as a commodity—just as you saw the children as such. They will use your genetically altered body as the next best source to exploit. You will be milked like a cow and bled like a patient in the Dark Ages."

"Not a very pretty prospect, Darlin'," Annabella told her lover. "The last thing I'd care to see is your yummy body poked, probed, dissected and squeezed dry."

Mersky's agile mind rapidly reassessed his position. He blocked those in the room from listening in, while he ran down several scenarios of escape. All ended in a blind, dark alley. Checkmate...for now, anyway.

"It's a difficult concept to grasp," Scott said. Mersky wondered if the young man, who he now suspected had been responsible for Spooner reversing her decision to upgrade him to commander, could read his blocked thoughts. "You are only recently departed from Earth and a life of privilege and power," Scott continued. "Among most civilized, cognitive life forms, that kind of primitive structure no longer exists."

"How do you know?" Mersky asked. "You've just left Earth yourself." Scott smiled.

"Not really, Mr. Mersky. We've been traveling out here for several years."

Annabella was surprised by Scott's statement. This was the first she had heard about it. Mersky had told her he had no idea why his processing to commander had been stopped by Spooner. Now she suspected that the children had something to do with it. She queried Ruth, but her Chief Commander's mind was blocked with her own thoughts.

Ruth was listening to Scott intently, remembering the display of projection the children had made to Antares and Klane. She had witnessed Melody, Scott and Beam project, but they had not explained how it had been accomplished. They did say more would be revealed when they reached Antares.

"Traveling out here for years while you remained on Earth?" Mersky said sarcastically. "Do you take me for a fool?" Scott just smiled and nodded.

"I think your plan to exploit was that of a fool. Look...we have all been granted a giant genetic leap. Maybe by accident. Maybe, as the Antareans believe, as part of The Master's Grand Plan. No matter. We know what we must do. In time, you too might come to understand the Universe, and your place in it." Mersky shuddered a bit as felt the power of the young man standing before him.

"The choice is yours," Ruth told Mersky. "Head Counsel Spooner said you may travel with the Brigade to a new assignment."

"On a probationary basis," Scott added.

"Annabella will be with you. If things work out, you may join the Brigade in the future," Ruth said.

Mersky glanced around at the room's Spartan furnishings. Artificial sunlight streamed through the window. Outside, was a holograph of his boyhood home, the hill country near Austin, Texas. He had enough contact with the Antareans to know they were an unemotional race, dedicated to their mission of spreading their Master's Grand Plan. He was a born-again Christian, and thus rejected any belief different from his own. Jesus Christ was the one and only savior, and the road to heaven meant total commitment to that belief. All others with different beliefs, he had learned and accepted, would be destroyed in the Rapture with the second coming of Christ. But that was on Earth. What would Jesus say about Antares, or the seemingly thousands of other planets and beings that the Antareans had encountered? Has Jesus visited all those places? Would the beings out there all be destroyed in the Rapture? Mersky's brain ached with questions. His body trembled with doubt.

"You have far to go, Mr. Mersky, and much to learn about the Universe," Scott told him. "Processing did not give you wisdom or tolerance."

"How is it possible that you read my thoughts?" Mersky asked. "I am blocking you."

"People like you, who wish to impose their will on others, cannot block those aspects of personality."

Scott's words went deep into Mersky as truth. A shiver of fear moved down Mersky's spine. "And if you choose to travel in space and meet other races, you will find your own narrow, parochial beliefs crumble like the walls of an ancient city whose time has long passed."

Mersky felt contempt for this boy lecturing him. He now knew that Scott Green, and not Ruth Charnofsky had somehow convinced Spooner to halt his upgrade to commander.

"Think about Earth, Mr. Mersky, so small, existing in a cosmos teeming with life. Think about your belief that only those like you will enter, what you call, the kingdom of heaven. On Earth, that means billions of people are doomed. Now think of the billions upon billions of beings who live in a universe unknown to fanatic religious leaders on Earth. Do you think there is a God who has fathered sons on all those planets? Do you think that your morality, your so-called values, your rituals, your taboos, your concept of God's word, is the only truth? Standing here, on a planet light years from your own, aware that life is everywhere, can you still believe that humans on Earth are the only living beings that your God and his Son care about? Is the rest of the Universe pagan and unworthy?"

Mersky felt his mind invaded by doubt. Was this boy the devil's messenger or, perhaps, the evil one himself?

"The older, wiser civilizations in the Universe, like the Antareans, learned long ago that religious fanatics use fear, myth and mysticism for only one purpose—to control others. Those who espouse 'only one true way' bring subjugation, misery and death. It is a murderous and selfish madness that can destroy all on Earth." Ruth and Annabella listened to the passionate young man with great pride. "I believe you are a test, Mr. Mersky," Scott continued. "A test as to whether all Earth-humans will be able to join the family of space travelers. Our hope is that you pass that test," Scott concluded.

In the silence that followed, Gideon Mersky began to examine his innermost motives. He felt as though he was opening a door to a far greater meaning of existence than any minister, priest, pope or president had ever envisioned. His attempt to use the powers of the children for his own personal gain seemed irrelevant, as the handsome young man standing before him suggested.

Ruth was now certain that this new race of Earth-humans, and all those who would follow, were destined to carry a special message throughout the Universe. Annabella Costa's take on what had transpired was a little different.

"You listen to that boy, Gideon. He's straight talkin' and wise beyond his years. You'd best get your act together quickly, Honey mine," she chided. Mersky's brow furrowed.

"I've listened. What's the rush?"

"The rush, Lamby-Pie, is 'cause I have a little appointment back on Earth in about eight months, and it would be real nice if y'all were there to hold my hand when our darlin' little son pops out to say hello, and thank you for his life. Fact is, he'll probably be a talkin' to us sooner than that."

CHAPTER THIRTY
WHAT WE ARE

A large area had been cleared for an unprecedented assembly in the Great Hall of Kinnear, close to the Earth exhibit. Seating for several hundred, divided into four sections, was installed around a raised center stage. It was crafted of the same forged, translucent magma as the floor. Unlike the floor, it was not lit from beneath.

The first section was occupied by the Lewises, Perlman's and Brigade members made up of the children's parents, and those who had remained on Antares after the gathering for inter-galactic training. Gideon Mersky sat with Annabella Costa in one of the uppermost rows. Brigade Chief Commander Ruth Charnofsky sat alone in the front of the section.

The second section held many Antareans from government, space exploration and trade. Among them were Commander Beam, recently returned from Klane, and Commander Alya Mark.

In the third section, the Antarean High Council and their aides occupied seats in order of their rank. Head Counsel Spooner sat alone in front. Ambassador/Counsel Amos Bright, also returned from Klane, sat in the row directly behind her.

The fourth section contained the children of Butterfly House, except the Erhardt twins and Laga Martindale who were back on Earth, and the three children who had been raised on their father's home-planets. Scott and Melody sat alone in the front of that section.

The phosphorescent Chorlian stone ceiling, normally glowing brightly from the light of Antarean heat-crystal chandeliers, was subdued. One chandelier, positioned directly over the stage, had been lowered. Its golden light spilled gently onto the audience. The stage remained dark. As the audience settled into silence, the setting resembled a theater in-the-round moments before a play was to begin.

Spooner rose to her full height. As she gracefully glided up the steps and onto the stage, her long diaphanous robes swept along behind her.

"With the destruction by an asteroid of Antares Quad-Three, our base on Earth, the Master did not reveal that we were soon to enter this new chapter of space exploration and trade. At the time, we mourned the loss of our base, and the cocooning of our diplomatic army." She turned toward the Brigade section. "And when a mission, led by Commander Amos Bright, returned to reclaim our army, we had no idea of The Master's plan for you, our Geriatric Brigade." Spooner bowed deeply toward the Brigade. Ruth rose and returned the bow. The entire section rose and bowed toward the Antarean leader. "When Counsel/Ambassador Bright brought you into our lives," Spooner continued, "little did we know how important you would become to our missions of trade and exploration. Not only did you replace the functions of our diplomatic army, you have endeared yourselves to many races and beings, including the Parmans, our inter-galactic Guides. Now, as we expand our missions to galaxies beyond, your extraordinary communication skills have become critical to our success. We welcome your partnership in this new and great endeavor of The Master's Grand Plan."

A hum of surprise, and some tacit approval, came from the Antarean section. Spooner then turned to the children. "And here are the newest Earth-humans to join us—the children of Butterfly House. They represent a giant evolutionary leap for the Earth-human race, and possess extraordinary powers. We welcome them to Antares, and to furthering the work of The Master's Grand Plan." Spooner bowed to the children and slowly clapped her hands, a gesture that was Earth-human, not Antarean. Her tribute was joined enthusiastically by the Brigade audience, then cautiously by the Antarean section and politely by the Antarean High Council. Then, as gracefully as Spooner had arrived, she left the stage. Scott and Melody stood and, holding hands, walked up the steps onto the stage.

"Thank you, Head Counsel Spooner," Scott began, "thank you, High Council and Antareans; thank you, parents; and thank you, Brigade members and commanders for your kind welcome to Antares. Our stay here will not be long." A murmur of surprise rippled through everyone in the audience. Melody moved forward.

"About nine years ago," she said, "we learned that it is not our destiny to travel and work with Antares, or the Geriatric Brigade. Our mission in the Universe is different from yours." Spooner stood and raised her hand, capturing the attention of the gathering.

"There is a misunderstanding," she said. "The purpose of this gathering is to welcome you to the only true mission—that of The Master. In this great hall, we are surrounded by proof of His Grand Plan. Here are represented the hundreds of planets and systems; the thousands of races and beings; the wonders of our galaxy that we have visited. It is irrefutable, living proof of The Master's Grand Plan." A loud, high-pitched wail of approval came from the Antarean section. "It was The Master who guided us to establish Antares Quad-Three on Earth," Spooner continued, moving around the stage as her voice grew louder and stronger. "It was The Master who sent the asteroid. It was The Master who had us form the Geriatric Brigade. It was The Master who gave back to your parents the gift of procreation and your conception. It was The Master who brought forth and gave you your gifts. It was The Master who gave you to us to use those gifts to spread word of His Grand Plan now, and even beyond our own galaxy. This you may not...you cannot, refute!"

A line of tension and confrontation in the Great Hall of Kinnear was suddenly, sharply drawn. The audience was hushed. The Antareans present had never seen or heard such an emotional outburst from their Head Counsel. The Brigade members and commanders were uneasy. What had the children done? Why had they waited until this moment to deny the Antareans most sacred mission and purpose?

"We can give you some insight into what we are, and what we must do, Head Counsel Spooner," Scott responded calmly, "but no one, including ourselves, can know our ultimate purpose or destination." The Antareans murmured their displeasure. Rising to her full height,

Spooner glided rapidly toward the stage, apparently to confront the two children directly.

"Please be patient, Head Counsel Spooner," Scott said, raising his hand to block her, "and take your seat. His tone of voice was polite, but firm. "Allow us to continue, and you will understand." Spooner hesitated for a moment, considering her options. She then reluctantly returned to her seat, but sat stiff and upright, ready to interrupt and announce the gathering closed.

"Thank you, Head Counsel Spooner," Scott said, as he moved to one side of the stage. Melody walked to the opposite side. The stage area darkened. Then an image began to form between them, and around them. The stage became the shore of a large lake. The land, foliage and water were tinted by the blue light of the dwarf star—Sparkle Plenty—the Life-Giver of the Aicha, on the planet Paccum, in the Manigra Galaxy. Scott and Melody walked toward a gathering of Aicha and their visitors—Brigade Commander Betty Franklin, the Brigade and Antarean landing party and Shai-Noa, the Antarean mission commander.

The Aicha children ran to greet Scott and Melody, squealing with excitement. Scott and Melody returned the greeting telepathically, but all in the Great Hall of Kinnear heard it.

"Ahhh," Halo, the Aicha exclaimed. "The children come again. Greetings, dear friends."

Betty Franklin and the rest of her landing party were dumbstruck. They saw no sign of a Mothership. The two had just appeared out of nowhere, millions of light years from Earth, Antares and The Milky Way Galaxy.

"Who are you?" Betty asked.

"I'm Scott Green. Mary and Ben's son."

"And I'm Melody Messina, Julia and Vincent's daughter."

"From Butterfly House? But how?"

"We have left Cayman Brac and, for the moment, dwell on Antares. Many there are observing us right now."

"It is what I told you," Halo, the Aichan leader, said to a confused Betty Franklin. "The children come and visit us. They are the ones who helped evolve our young in-egg."

"You said watching us? Who?" Betty asked.

"Aunt Ruth, my parents, the Perlmans, the Lewises, many of the Brigade," Scott answered.

"And Head Counsel Spooner, Counsel Bright...in fact, the entire Antarean High Council and many Antareans," Melody added.

"How is this possible?" Shai-Noa asked.

"We have the ability to project ourselves to far away places," Melody answered.

"We do not want to disturb you," Scott said to Betty.

"This projection is a way for us to begin to explain to the Antareans, our parents, and the Brigade, who and what we are, and what we must do."

Those gathered in the Great Hall of Kinnear were silent, awed by the vision on the stage. Those parents and commanders, and Spooner, who had personally witnessed the children's projecting before this display, were stunned by their ability to reach across hundreds of millions of light-years to other galaxies. Then Scott and Melody said goodbye to the landing party and the Aicha and their young, promising to return and visit soon.

"And you may speak to us whenever you wish," Scott told the Aicha young as they gathered around him. "We love you. We wish you peace and long life."

Melody and Scott began to fade, as did Paccum, until the stage in the Great Hall of Kinnear was again dark. Only Scott and Melody remained. Ruth rose and spoke first.

"You did not tell us you were able to project to other galaxies. What else have you kept from us?" In hearing anger in Ruth's voice, Spooner felt, for the first time since the Antareans had to rely on the Brigade commanders for communications, that they were loyal and to be trusted.

"And where else have you meddled in the evolution of others?" Spooner added, as she stood to her full height.

"We have not meddled," Scott said firmly.

"Really, Scott?" Ruth chided him. "What about the Sloor on Klane, and these young Aicha?"

"They evolved," Beam Amato answered from her seat among the children.

DAVID SAPERSTEIN

"You say..." Ruth turned toward Beam. "Both races have been altered away from their phylum, toward mammalian. Both say it happened when you visited their young before birth. We saw that when you projected to Klane, and just now on Paccum. That cannot be denied."

At that moment, all the children stood, and silently filed out of their seats, onto the stage, joining Scott and Melody. The unoccupied center of the stage grew very dark. And then, in a flash of bright light, the Erhardt twins and Laga Martindale appeared. A second flash brought Autumn, the daughter of Ruth and Panatoy, from the planet Rigel. She was followed by José, the oldest son of Brigade member Karen Moreno, and Tommachkikla, a miner from the planet Destero. Finally, Ilena, the daughter of Brigade member Ellie-Mae Boyd, and Dr. Manterid, a chemist from the planet Betch, appeared. All three showed features of both parents, but favored their fathers more. Now, gathered on the stage, were all the children of Brigade members born on mother-planet Earth sixteen years ago.

"You will have the answers to your questions now," Scott announced. Awed, Ruth and Spooner sat down. Autumn blew her mother a kiss.

"Let us first address the accusations of blasphemy and meddling," Scott began. "We have never meddled."

"Then explain the Sloor and the Aicha!" Amos Bright shouted as he stood, pointing a slender, blue finger. His tone was accusatory. "They clearly stated that it was you, the children, who caused the changes in their young."

"Yes. But we have only projected to where we were invited," Scott responded.

"Never to where we were unwelcome," Melody added, pointing at Amos Bright. "Our abilities came to us because you caused genetic changes in our parents, and we became a new race. Is what you did meddling?" she asked rhetorically.

"Of course not," Scott answered before Bright could respond. "You would say it was unforeseen, or necessary for space travel, or simply part of The Master's Grand Plan. But the fact is, it happened," Scott continued, "and we are what we are, in part, because of what you did.

Do not blame us for what we are. We do not consider it meddling or blasphemy."

"We do not blame for what you are," Spooner then said. "It is for what you do that is our concern."

"And what is that?" Scott asked. "We are summoned by other beings. We hear their calls, their cries, their prayers, their wishes. We cannot tune them out. And so we respond."

"It is that response that we question," Spooner said.

"They ask who we are; where we are; what we are. We speak truthfully. They invite us to meet. We join them. To teach. This mostly happens before birth, or hatching, or dividing. It causes cognitive capacity to expand. And, as in beings like the Sloor and Aicha, it results in genetic change, and sometimes evolutionary leaps. We don't completely understand why." Scott faced the Antarean section and the High Council. "You apply everything in this Universe to The Master. That is your belief. It is what anchors your civilization, and holds it fast. It has served you well and you are honored in our galaxy." He then faced Ruth and the Brigade. "You brought us into being. You serve with the Antareans on their missions. You have seen a galaxy teeming with life. You are of great value to that work, and we are proud of you. We have seen that many of our home-planet's inhabitants murder, oppress and enslave in the name of their respective God and gods. Their tradition is steeped in meddling and blasphemy. You and we are no longer like them."

"You are cynical for ones so young," Ruth said softly.

"No, Aunt Ruth. Not cynical. We have been privileged to see truth. We know where we came from; where we are going and what we must do. You see, there is more to tell."

Once again, the stage grew dark. This time, all of the children began to fade into a large chamber of the main government building on Liast, in the Bezzolentine Galaxy. Frank and Andrea Hankinson, several Brigade members, Antarean Commander Duartone and his Antarean crew, were seated at a long table across from Shinner, the Liastan city leader; Tellic, from the Liastan central government; and more than a dozen off-planet visitors. The table and chairs had been specially constructed to accommodate the various sizes and shapes of those gathered there. All wore universal translating devices, except the children, who also appeared in the chamber. They were immediately recognized by the Liastan leaders, Shinner and Tellic.

"We are gathered as you requested," Shinner stated, as he raised his massive head and spread his antennae.

"We greet you in peace, children of Butterfly House," Tellic added, as he too showed respect.

The children filed along either side of the table, bowing until all had been greeted. All, except the Brigade members, knew the children. Scott stood next to Frank Hankinson, and Melody next to Shinner.

"I am Scott Green, and this is Melody Messina. We are from Butterfly House, as Tellic said."

You are your father's son," Frank said and he took Scott's hand and shook it. "We were told by the Liastans that a surprise was coming."

"Many on Antares are observing us now," Scott stated. "The Antareans hold deep religious beliefs that our Universe is controlled by an entity; The Master and His Grand Plan. They have traveled our galaxy, and now have come to yours. They have rules they live by. Good rules. Fair rules. One is to never meddle in the affairs of any beings or planets. To do so, they say, is to deny The Master's Plan."

"And your parents also believe this?" Shinner asked.

"We are not sure," Melody answered. "The Brigade is partnered with Antares at present. Although they may hold differing Earthly beliefs regarding the creation of the Universe, they have agreed to serve The Master's Plan."

"And they accuse you of breaking their rules?" Shinner asked.

"Yes."

"But it was we who called out to you," Tellic said.

"Perhaps you would like to tell how we first came to know Liast," Melody suggested.

"The invitation came from our own young, as it did from many," Tellic responded. "Everyone here knows, as we have learned from you of Butterfly House, the unborn everywhere are part of each other. They possess a strong common bond—the wonder of a life becoming.

As they develop physically, in womb, or egg, or cell, or crystal, they know a powerful universal language, a common tongue transmitted by thought."

A murmur spread throughout the audience in the Great Hall of Kinnear. None present could recall such an event in their lives.

"Yes. All unborn have the potential to communicate with other species and living forms throughout the Universe," Melody confirmed. "But for most, this reality is lost at birth, because they are born into societies and civilizations whose rules, laws and customs are not grounded in universal truths, but rather narrow, myopic views of their place in the Universe, or, at times, grandiose ones. That language and means to communicate is forgotten. Yet a precious few do remember, and they are driven to fulfill a special destiny. They strive to keep the promise given before birth—to visit one another, to help all, to bring peace. That is who we are, and what we are."

A Sakeous, called Tia-Ron, rose to speak next. Sakeous are a warm-blooded, carbon-based reptilian race from a planetary system across the Bezzolentine Galaxy, one-hundred-six million light-years away. Their planet is called Morihach-4. They, like the other non-Liastans present, have been space travelers for a very long time. They were one of the first to visit Liast.

"In the process of communicating with Liastans, we Sakeous learned that their unborn not only communicated with these visitors, but were exposed to their genetics. In our case, when contact was made on Morihach-4, we learned that those developing in-egg chose to borrow, to share, some of the genetic characteristics of their visitors. They were not forced. The children from Butterfly House did not meddle in evolution. Parts of the genetic material that they carried, when asked, was shared. But only when asked!"

One by one, the visitors from other planets and galaxies spoke of the children's visits, and how grateful they were that they had met their young. The story was the same. The children never meddled, but they did, from time to time, when asked, share genes.

On Antares, the previously charged atmosphere of confrontation and condemnation slowly changed to understanding, and then to awe.

The Brigade members and commanders were very emotional about the children. The Antareans were calmed. Secretly, they congratulated Spooner and Amos Bright for their initial decision to process the Earth-human seniors and bring them to Antares. That act, for them, confirmed The Master's Grand Plan.

The last to speak at the meeting table on Liast were two humanoids with dark green, bark-like skin. They had two sets of eyes; one set aimed forward, and one that moved within a milky, viscous fluid, along the perimeter of their perfectly round heads. Several antennae protruded from their long necks. The taller of the two moved next to Scott, and put an appendage, a thin stiff arm with a flat, paddle-like end, around the young man's shoulder.

"We are called Fougarden," he said, addressing the audience on Antares as though he could see them. And he could. "I am called Thist—a seeker. I am like your children with memory of time before birth and contact with other species in this Universe. We have been space travelers for as long as we have memory." His voice, filtered through a translator device, was deep, yet soft and soothing, sounding like a kindly minister addressing his Sunday morning flock. "We are evolved," Thist continued, "in a galaxy close to the very edge of this Universe...a very old galaxy. We are a race that, like you Antareans, explore and trade. This is our work and our way. Our young came to know the children of Butterfly House when both were unborn. They readily shared genetic material. Both our young and yours made evolutionary leaps." He bent over and whispered something in Scott's ear. Scott nodded. "We believe the children of Butterfly House, and our own young, now possess, reassembled, the basic genetics of the first alive; the ones from which all cognitive life evolved. To know these children, yours and ours, is to have a glimpse of what was, what is, and what will become, in our Universe." The Fougarden said no more.

The audience in the Great Hall of Kinnear watched silently as the children bid farewell to those gathered in the chamber on Liast. The image faded until the stage was dark. And then, out of the darkness, all the children reappeared.

"Now you understand," Scott said. "Contact and change came by invitation from the unborn, the unspoiled and pure. In that state, we know one another, and we are the same, unfinished but becoming. In that state of existence, many choices are made. This is how all evolved. This is how it has always been."

"With processing, random genetic mixing, and visits from the Fougarden unborn," Melody stated, "we are a new race on our own mission."

Ruth and Spooner stood again. Both walked up onto the stage. They were of one mind, and spoke in one voice.

"We understand. We apologize. We accept. We wish you long life and success. Go in peace, and remember us."

The children left the stage to find their parents, Ruth found her daughter Autumn, and embraced her.

"Does your father know?" she asked.

"Yes. He gave me his blessing, too. I promise I will not be a stranger. None of us will. We love you all very much."

The Fougarden spacecraft was huge. It dwarfed the latest Antarean Mothership. Its shimmering skin was more liquid than solid. There was no visible means of propulsion; no engines, drives or Parman type Guides. It hovered 150 miles above Antares' frozen surface.

Final good-byes were said outside the Probeship that would take the children up to the awaiting Fougarden craft. The Erhardt twins and Laga had returned to Earth. The parents, who had only spent a few days with their children, were understandably sad. But now they knew there would be regular contact, long life, and the prospect of visits in the future. There was even some joking about their soon becoming grandparents. The off-planet children who had not grown up at Butterfly House were now part of the group. Everyone lingered, touching, hugging, kissing, promising...

And then it was time to board the Probeship. With long, tight embraces, wishes of safe voyage, blessings and tears, the Brigade children, a new race, were on their way to destinations and a future unknown.

The hatch of the Probeship was sealed. It slowly moved into the launch tube that would catapult it to the Antarean surface. The tube sealed shut. A loud whoosh of compressed gas propelled the Probeship up to the planet's surface where its engines engaged and launched out into the void. The vessel's pilot, Amos Bright, locked into the vector coordinates to rendezvous with the Fougarden inter-galactic craft in orbit high above Antares.

Spooner and Ruth left the spaceport together. Both understood that they had experienced something very special in knowing the children.

"It is good that Amos is the one to pilot them from Antares," Ruth said.

"Yes. He requested that honor, and I was joyful to grant it. It closes a circle," Spooner said. She paused. "Are you sorry that he brought you out from Earth?" she asked.

"Of course not," Ruth answered quickly. "Not one of us feels that way. We talked about it last night with the children. No, Head Counsel Spooner. We are delighted with our work, and our lives. Are you sorry we came?"

"Not at all, my dear friend Ruth." Spooner touched Ruth's shoulder. It was a familiarity that Spooner had never used. They began to walk again. The children have changed Antares, Ruth thought. "Scott Green privately told me something very profound," Spooner then said. "You are advanced, he said, but chose to stop your evolution by cloning instead of mixing genetically, and by doing so, you advance only technically. But you advanced our parents, perhaps unknowingly, and that, in turn, brought us forth. That is how we believe the Universe works, he told me. Actions cause change; change causes advancement; advancement causes growth..."

"Maybe that's right, But advancement and growth toward what?" Ruth asked.

"That is what Commanders Alya Mark and Beam also wonder. Perhaps Antares will investigate that question by experimenting with a return to genetic mixing." Spooner's thin lips widened. Was that a smile, Ruth wondered. "Who knows?" Spooner mused. "Perhaps we might even find that emotion you call love."

"Yes," Ruth said softly. "You might. But what might that do to your belief in The Master's Grand Plan?" Spooner stopped and put her thin blue hand on Ruth's shoulder again.

"Nothing can change that belief, only perhaps its name." They walked a little farther to the elevator that would take them down three miles to the city. "There are other questions I would like to have answered, Ruth."

"Yes?"

"Where will the children go? What will they do? What will they become?"

"I don't know," Ruth answered. "But I suspect, in time, we will find out. What I wonder most of all is what might the future generations of these children be?"

EPILOGUE

The children of Butterfly House, with their counterparts from the Fougarden, dispersed across the galaxies in pre-determined pairings. They were to be mates for life. Their offspring would make even greater evolutionary leaps, and influence many species and races in this Universe.

The Geriatric Brigade continued to work with the Antareans, exploring many other galaxies. Every few years, fifty or so women, with their mates, returned to home-planet Earth to bear their young. The unborn blended their genes with other races. While the people of Earth struggled to survive and cleanse their planet, Butterfly House flourished, and its secret was kept. The new children were nourished, taught, and grew there. And when their time came, they too moved out among the stars with mates.

The Fougarden, whose galaxy was on the very edge of our Universe, had made an incredible discovery that they shared with the children. In what seemed an infinite void beyond their own galaxy, they had discovered the existence of the Universes. In other words, a Multiverse. There were billions of them, containing trillions of stars, quadrillions of planets, moons, asteroids, and upon them, sextillions of races and species. From the tiniest particles of an atom—electrons, protons, neutrons, quarks, all rotating around a nucleus, to the vastness of endless space, there was matter, infinite matter, churning in a void without end—becoming, heating, cooling, growing, combining, changing, dying, beginning. It was a never-ending cycle without boundary or containment that was there and had been there for all time.

Everything in it, alive or inanimate, was part of everything else. Everything changes. Nothing is lost. Nothing is destroyed. Nothing is wasted. Nothing, including time and space, ever ends. It goes on and on.

The children of Butterfly House, and their descendants, understood that their mission was to travel to the Multiverse. Before they left on their journey, Scott and Melody, now mates for life, sent a message back to the Brigade, Antares and Butterfly House.

"We are all; everything and everyone, made of the same. We are stardust. At this moment, in time and space, we are in a form that is a gift. It is called life—precious and glorious. But we will end, die, and this form we now possess will again become stardust. And then, perhaps in time, which is endless, the stardust that once was us will become a part of life again. It will not know past or future. It, too, will begin and end. We are all, forever, part of what IS, and that is our gloriously endless journey. There is nothing else."